BY THE SAME AUTHOR

Ironbound Island
Marty Runs Away to Sea
Meg and Melissa
Meg of Heron's Neck
Meg's Mysterious Island
A Mystery for Meg
Treasure on Heron's Neck
Trouble on Heron's Neck

ELIZABETH LADD

# The Indians on the Bonnet

ILLUSTRATED BY RICHARD CUFFARI

NEW YORK
WILLIAM MORROW AND COMPANY

Printed in the United States of America.
Library of Congress Catalog Card Number 75-154974
Design by Cynthia Basil.
Weekly Reader Children's Book Club Edition

# CONTENTS

# The Indians on the Bonnet

# CHAPTER ONE

# January Storm

The gale howling around the corner of the house awoke Jess. His first thought was, rain! In January! It can't be! But rain it was, pounding against the window.

"When did it start, Grandma?" Jess was pulling on his shirt as he dashed into the kitchen.

"Right after midnight, and the storm's been picking up ever since. You better go out and make sure the window hasn't blown out of the hen house. We don't want all the hens to drown."

"Can't I eat first?" The delicious smell of bacon curled through the room.

"Not until you tend to the animals. Put on oilskins when you go out, and take that dog with you."

Jess did not protest. He had grown up on a farm, and he knew that the animals always come first, even if the Mannings now owned only a dozen red hens and a speckled cow. And, of course, Tatters, the raggedy, tattered, strawberry-blond dog, who was Jess's best friend.

Jess put on his rubber boots and oilskins and grabbed the milk pail. "Try not to get too much water in the milk," Grandmother said, as he pushed Tatters outdoors. Tatters hated rain as much as a cat does, but once outside, she accepted it and ran on to the barn with Jess.

The gale was a real humdinger, Jess realized, as soon as he was out of the house. All the snow had vanished, and water spread in a silver sheet over the frozen earth. The wind made a high-pitched shriek as it tore through the cedars against the sound of the heavy pounding of surf on the rocky shore beyond the house.

The wind and the rain almost blinded Jess, but he clutched the milk pail and staggered along. A piece of tar paper wrenched from the hen-house roof went past him, rolling over and over as if it had a life of its own.

Jess was relieved to reach the shelter of the barn, a warm, dark place, smelling of hay and cow. Tatters ducked in gratefully and began licking her big, spongy feet. Jess fed the cow, got out the three-legged stool, and milked her quickly and efficiently. As he had been doing this chore since he was five, and now he was almost thirteen, his fingers moved automatically.

While working, he was thinking about the storm. It was one of those very high tides called a spring tide, and the water would be at its highest point at noon. What kind of flotsam would wash onto their beach? Some nice planks, boards, or siding perhaps. He must go to the shore as soon as it stopped raining.

Grandmother Manning's only income was a pension, and since Jess had come to live with her, he had become aware of how much things cost. Why, they had built the shed that housed the hens from boards they had picked up on the beach. Finding these treasures before somebody else did was essential.

When Jess returned to the house, breakfast was waiting. While Tatters curled up on her blanket, Jess sat down to bacon, eggs, toast, and fresh milk. Sheltered by the great trees, the house seemed safe from the storm.

"Everything was all right," Jess said, biting into a slice of toast. "A piece of paper's blown off the hen house, but I can fix it when the wind stops. The hens don't mind. They're in a dry corner."

"We're lucky if a piece of paper is all we've lost," Grandmother said. "In a storm like this, I think of the people who are out on the water. Imagine all the boats and lobster traps and gear that will be lost."

On the Maine coast, these were the worries people had during every bad storm, Jess had learned. "I bet a lot of things will wash up in Knowlton's Cove," he said. "Could I go and take a look?"

"In this storm? You were soaked just going to the barn."

"I mean, after it stops raining," Jess explained.

"You could go tomorrow," his grandmother said.

"But somebody may get there first. Remember how the Jenkins boy got all those nice pine boards just because I never got there in time to pick them up and throw them on the banking?" An unwritten law was that anything one picked up at the tide line and threw on the banking belonged to him. No one would touch it before the finder carried it away.

"Well, we'll see. I don't like to have you around the shore alone when the sea is breaking like this."

"Grandma, you know I'm careful!" Jess insisted.

By noon the rain had stopped, and the wind shifted northwest. In a wild-looking sky pale, gray clouds scudded under a black storm cloud. Grandmother gave him permission to go, saying, "Don't stay too long, Jess. The sea is so rough you probably won't be able to pick up anything."

Jess put on his rubber boots and heavy jacket and whistled to Tatters. Knowlton's Cove was not far, less than a quarter of a mile of traveling on an old, brush-grown field and dirt road. The wind still roared far overhead in the tops of the big trees, and the road was littered with fallen cones and small branches. Twice Jess saw trees that had been uprooted by the storm and lay like fallen giants.

As they neared the water, the roar of the sea became deafening. Only a thin screen of alders hid the cove. Tatters had been running about gaily, searching for squirrels, but now she returned and followed Jess uneasily. Water the color of mud was boiling over the blue clay banking, tearing out great chunks of earth. The undertow hurled small stones and boulders like tossed dice. Old logs and trees wallowed in the surf, battering against the banking and the alders.

Jess saw in a glance that searching the beach without getting soaked was impossible. Grandmother was right; nothing could be gotten today. Then suddenly he spotted a small skiff, rolling sideways in the surf only a few feet from shore. I can reach it, Jess thought.

As the boat was some distance down the beach, and walking on the shore was impossible, Jess went back to the road and attempted to push his way through the alders abreast of the boat. Tatters ran before him, barking loudly. When Jess pushed through the last of the trees, he was astonished to see that someone else had reached the boat first. A boy, smaller than Jess, wearing a red jacket, rubber boots, and dungarees was struggling to retrieve it in the surf. He held the skiff with one hand, and in the other he grasped a stick of driftwood, which he hurled at the barking dog. Tatters ran from him, yelping.

Furious, Jess yelled, "What are you doing—" Then he saw that the boy was in serious trouble. Although he was not strong enough to hold the skiff against the battering waves, he clung to it like a limpet and the undertow was pulling him off his feet.

Jess plunged down the banking and into the surf. He grasped the bow of the skiff and

steadied it enough for the boy to regain his footing. The water was so cold it burned like fire. When Jess had a chance to get his first good look at the boy, he was shocked. He had the brownest skin Jess ever had seen and long black hair, which fell to his shoulders and was sticky with spray.

"Come on," Jess shouted. "If we pull together, we can get her up."

The boy snarled, showing teeth as white as Tatters', and his eyes were like bits of coal. "You let go! It's mine!"

"You fool! Come on, pull!" Jess's boots were full of water, and his feet were growing numb with cold. The boy said no more, and somehow between them they dragged the skiff into the alders beyond the reach of the tide.

"It'll be safe now. You can get it tomorrow," Jess said, taking off his boots and dumping out the water. He was so chilled his teeth chattered. "We'd better get home fast. Where do you live?" Suddenly he realized that his companion was a girl! The jacket, dungarees, and rubber boots had fooled him.

She was shaking as hard as Jess, and her brown skin had turned blue. "Come on." Jess caught her arm. "Run, and we'll get warm." They stumbled through the alders and up the road. "You're going home with me."

"No, I live that way." The girl gestured vaguely toward the north.

Running up the old road had warmed them, but now they were panting. "Who are you?" Jess asked. "I never saw you before."

"I'm Cory. I live on the Bonnet."

Jess understood. "Why, you're one of those Injuns," he said.

Cory stared at him with eyes like black buttons. "We don't like you to call us that."

"I'm sorry." Jess had not intended to offend her, but he often had heard this term used. "You're coming home with me. Grandma will dry you out. The Bonnet's a mile away. You'll freeze before you get there."

"I'm used to the cold. Besides, your dog'll bite me, and you tried to take that boat away from me."

"I didn't. I was just trying to help you," Jess insisted. "Tatters barks, but she wouldn't hurt anyone."

"I don't need any of your old help," the girl said, but she followed him.

Jess was freezing and figured that Cory must be just as cold. He noticed that she kept up with him and made no effort to turn north. Curiosity gnawed at him. The Bonnet was a point of high land, covered with pine and spruce, and old, rundown fields. Once it had been owned by a wealthy family, and in those days, long before Jess was born, it had looked very different. The owner had built a house, as large as a small hotel, near what the towns-people called Backside Cove.

After he died, the Bonnet changed hands many times. News in town was that the present owner had hired a caretaker to stay there this winter. An Indian! A real Indian! What was he like? Where did he come from? Very little information seeped out from the Bonnet, however, for the Indian kept to himself.

Grandmother Manning was a sensible woman, and when the children burst in the house, soaking wet and half frozen, she didn't waste time with words. In a few minutes both youngsters were wrapped in blankets, toasting beside the wood stove, while their clothing steamed on a line extending across the kitchen. They both were given bowls of hot corn chowder to eat.

Jess poured out the story of finding the skiff. "It's Cory's, you know. She found it first. She's an Injun, I mean, an Indian. She lives over on the Bonnet." Cory said nothing, but ate like a starved tiger.

"To what tribe do you belong?" Grandmother asked.

The black eyes rested on her for a long moment. "The Passamaquoddy."

"That's a long way north of here. Aren't you ever lonely, away from your friends?"

Cory swallowed a mouthful of stew. "Papa and I do all right."

"It must be hard on your mother."

The black eyes looked up again. "Ma's dead."

"Oh, I'm sorry," Grandmother said.

"It's all right. She died nine years ago, when I was born. Papa's got this good job now, and we get along just fine."

Cory's clothes were dry by the time they had finished the corn chowder. "It's a long way over to the Bonnet," Grandmother said. "Sure you don't want Jess to go with you?"

"No." Cory shook her head. Then she turned to Jess and said awkwardly, "Thank you for helping me with the skiff. I'm sorry I hit the dog."

"Oh, that's okay. It didn't hurt Tatters. I'll be seeing you again, won't I?"

"Maybe," Cory answered.

# CHAPTER TWO

# Mr. Raven

The snow came with February. The west wind mourned as it whipped around the house and fumbled with icy fingers at the windows. Great drifts formed in the garden, and over them snowbirds, like brown-flecked flakes of snow, fluttered hunting for old weed stocks. At last there came a day that was fair and mild. The cloudless, deep-blue sky seemed to rest on the earth. It was a day no one could stay indoors. Jess decided to go rabbit hunting.

One of the nicest things about Grandmother was the fact that she seldom said, "No." She would think the matter over, and if it was impractical, she would say so, but almost always she let Jess make his own decisions.

Jess found his grandmother hanging out the wash, the clean clothes blowing in the sun. When he spoke of rabbit hunting, she was silent for a minute. "Tatters isn't a hound, you know."

"Yes, but she'll chase a rabbit. She'll chase anything."

"A gun is good for just one thing, killing. So be careful with it."

"I know how to handle a rifle. You know that."

His grandmother sighed. The little .22 had been Jess's last present from his father, who had taught him how to use it. "All right, go if you want to, but be back before dark."

Jess went down the road, whistling, his rifle over his shoulder. Tatters ran happily ahead. The high ridges of snow thrown up by the plow had left the road in cold, blue shadow.

The road to the Bonnet, though, was unplowed, and not a track marked its purity. It would be just the place to hunt, Jess thought. He never would find a rabbit on the main road, but on the Bonnet, where no one hunted, there would be plenty of game. Rabbits would abound in blowdowns, and deer in the cedar swamp. Even fox would be plentiful.

Of course, there was a sign reading *No Trespassing, Order of Mr. J. Barnes,* nailed up at the entrance of the road. But what difference did it make? Mr. Barnes was far away in sunny Florida. The Indian caretaker was there, but ever since he had helped Cory with the skiff, Jess felt that he knew them well. Besides, the Bonnet covered forty acres, so there wasn't any need to hunt too close to the house they were living in at Backside Cove.

He turned onto the untouched road. The snow was not too deep, for great trees sheltered it. "Tatters, you watch out for a rabbit," he warned.

The road wound uphill, and on either side the spruces and cedars shut out the sun. It was cold and very still; not even a chickadee moved. Jess was tired and a little discouraged. He had walked half a mile and seen nothing. Even Tatters' energy had disappeared, and from time to time she sat down and tried to pull off the snowballs that had formed on the bottom of her large, furry paws.

Jess was thinking of turning back when he saw, by the break in the woods ahead, that they were reaching the top of a long hill. A few more steps, and he was in a wide clearing, where white fields spread out, rimmed with birches. Beyond them was the sea, a very dark blue, dotted with white ice cakes. There was something free and bright about this glimpse of the sea after the dark woods. Tatters began sniffing in the snow.

By this time Jess had given up looking for tracks, but Tatters seemed to have found something. Jess went ahead and looked. A rabbit! There was no mistaking that triple track.

The animal wasn't really a rabbit; it was a hare, which is larger. Since in winter its fur becomes white, to blend with the snow, and in summer turns brown, it is sometimes called the varying hare. Its big, flat feet are heavily furred, so that it can walk on the deep snow without sinking in, and for that reason another name for it is snowshoe hare.

Jess, though, referred to it as a rabbit, and said, "Tatters, you old rabbit hound! Go get him!"

Tatters galloped across the field, not baying, for she was not a real hound, but giving a yelp once in a while. Although Jess never had been hunting, he knew that a hare runs in a circle when chased by a dog. All the hunter has to do is to wait for it to go past him, and then he shoots it. Jess went to a spot on the edge of the woods.

There he heard the first stirring of life. Chickadees were busy in an old spruce, *dee-deeing* as they worked. A black-and-white woodpecker hammered loudly in the top of a birch, and a red squirrel was busy gathering spruce cones. Far overhead a flock of purple finches kept up a soft twittering as they bobbed past, and down on the shore a raven called. There was no sign of a hare, however.

Jess's feet were cold from standing in the snow. Even though the days grew longer in February, he had to remember to be home by dark. Suddenly Tatters began barking a very long way off, down at the end of the point. The hare must be doing all the wrong things, or else Tatters had lost the trail and was chasing something else.

Jess whistled, but Tatters continued barking. She must have treed something, a squirrel perhaps. Disgusted, Jess started to follow her trail, but walking was more difficult than he had anticipated. Wind had swept across the field all winter, gathering the snow of many storms into mammoth drifts. The curved mounds were compressed solid enough to support a hare and, in most cases, Tatters, but not Jess.

He floundered on, sometimes up to his knees in snow, whistling now and then. The dog was still far away, and the going was so bad that reaching her and getting back home would take a long time. Suddenly Jess thought, Tatters might return if he fired the gun. Hadn't he read that hunters used this method to recall their dogs, or was it something one did when he was lost? Jess couldn't remember. He wasn't sure what Tatters would do, for she never had heard a gun, but he fired carefully into the sky.

The little rifle made a terrible noise in the white stillness. It awoke a hundred crows, who must have been dozing in the woods at the end of the Bonnet. Screaming and cursing, the black flock departed. A few ravens added their hoarse comments to the general racket.

In a minute Tatters appeared, coming out of the woods in long bounds. Jess was pleased with her obedience, but he scolded her just the same. "Why didn't you come when I whistled? What happened to that rabbit?" Tatters peered at him fearfully from under the heavy thatch of her eyebrows, and then on a run she started for the road and home.

On the edge of the woods, in the direction from which Tatters had come, a man appeared. He began to move toward Jess, walking with smooth, easy strides, for he was wearing snowshoes.

Jess's first thought was to run. Perhaps that *No Trespassing* sign meant what it said. Then he realized that would be foolish. He only would flounder in the snow, and the man could catch him easily enough. So he stood his ground, and said, "Hello."

The man was tall, and in his plaid jacket, khaki pants, and heavy boots, he looked huge. His hair was hidden under an old wool cap, but his skin was the color of mahogany and his eyes like Cory's black buttons. Jess guessed that he was the Indian caretaker.

The man looked down at him. "You cannot read?"

"I'm sorry. I didn't mean any harm."

"You read sign, come on place, chase animals, shoot gun. Then you say, 'I didn't mean any harm.' "

Another person was coming out of the woods, also on snowshoes. "Cory!" Jess yelled. "It's me, Jess Manning."

Cory did not answer. She was walking with the peculiar stride of an experienced snow-shoer, following her father's path, and she came up behind him.

"Is this the boy you spoke about, the one who helped with the boat?" the man asked.

"Yes," answered Cory.

"We heard the dog barking, so we went to see. He had chased Cory's cat up a tree. Then we heard a shot."

Cory said, "It's all right. Jet's come down and run home."

"What are you hunting?" the Indian asked Jess.

"Not cats. I'm awfully sorry, Mr.—"

"The name is Raven."

"—Mr. Raven. I was rabbit hunting, and

Tatters was on a rabbit track, but she isn't a real hound. She will chase cats, but she never hurts them," he added hastily. "I wasn't shooting at anything. I just fired into the sky, hoping to call Tatters back."

"Hum. What would you have done with a rabbit?"

"Grandma would have made a stew."

"You like rabbit stew?"

"I never had any."

"You come home and eat with us. What do we have on the stove, Cory?"

The girl's face lighted up with a charming smile. "Rabbit stew! Very good rabbit stew! Come on, Jess. We'd like to have you."

"But Grandma will worry. She told me to be home before dark."

"You will be. We do things very quickly when we want to."

The two pairs of snowshoes pressed down the snow, so that it formed a firm path on which Jess could walk quite easily. "What about Tatters?" he asked.

"The dog? She will run home like the cat. Cats and dogs know the way home," the Indian said.

Snowshoe trails led in all directions in the birch woods. The Ravens must be out every day, although they never walked up to the main road. The dark house at Backside Cove was enormous, set among huge, black spruces. The afternoon sun touched the vacant windows with a baleful glare, and Jess shivered, not wholly from cold.

The Ravens lived in the servants' quarters, a couple of rooms in the right wing of the great house. The kitchen was scorching hot from the burning chunks of wood in the old iron stove. The room was cluttered with clothes, a saw, an axe, a pair of oars, and a shotgun, among other things, but it had a friendly, homelike warmth. The stew in the big pot smelled delicious.

Cory and her father left their snowshoes stuck in a snowbank by the door, and in the kitchen everyone pulled off their jackets and boots. Cory found a ladle and tin bowls. At the sound of "Meow!" in a loud, demanding voice, Mr. Raven opened the door, and in strode a short-haired, coal-black cat with a long tail. He had big ears, small, delicate paws, and a heart-shaped face with an aristocratic nose and golden eyes.

"There now, Jet." Cory gave him a ladleful of stew in one of the bowls. "Things are all right now."

## CHAPTER THREE

# A Short Visit

The stew was very good, thick and rich with plenty of meat. Cory dumped a package of flat, white crackers called pilot bread onto a plate, and they ate them with the stew.

"Why are you called Cory?" Jess asked between mouthfuls. "It doesn't sound Indian."

Cory's black eyes glowed at him. "What do you mean?"

"I thought Indians always had names of plants or birds or animals."

"You think maybe I should be called Little Skunk Cabbage?"

"Well, no."

"Besides, look at your name—Jesse. It sounds just like a girl's name!"

Jess turned red. "It's not! Jesse Manning is a name that's been in our family for a hundred years!"

"Her mother named her," Mr. Raven interrupted. "She gave her the name of the Sister, Cordelia, who cared for her when Cory was born. The name never fit her, so I called her Cory."

"My mother and father are both dead," Jess said. "They were killed three years ago in an auto accident. I've been living with Grandma ever since." Then Jess asked, his curiosity bubbling over, "How do you happen to be living here?"

"You mean, how did they let us off the reservation?"

"Well, yes." Jess blushed.

"We go anywhere we can find work," Mr. Raven said with dignity. "But few white men hire Indians. Mr. Barnes was wise. He was different. When he bought this place last summer, he saw that he needed a man willing to live like this." He indicated the two rooms with a sweep of his hand. "He needed someone who would get his own wood, stay on the place, look after things. So he came to the reservation and said he would hire an Indian."

"I like it here," Cory said.

"Good job," her father agreed. "The Sisters wanted Cory to stay with them, but I want my daughter with me."

"Sisters?" Jess did not understand.

"The holy nuns." Cory reached under her shirt and drew out a tiny cross that hung around her neck. "They taught me how to read and write."

"Oh." Jess stared. The Ravens not only were Indians, they were Catholic as well, the first Catholics he ever had known.

"How do you get to the store?" Jess asked at last. "I didn't see any tracks coming out."

"That was why I wanted the boat," Cory said. "There's a pair of oars here. Now we can row across the harbor to the store, that is, as long as there is no ice. But we don't go to the store much."

Her father explained, "Mr. Barnes gave us some money when he brought us here, and he said he'd send the wages every month, but we never heard from him again. He's in Florida, and I guess he's so busy there he forgot about the money. But you can't buy things without money."

"Couldn't you find work somewhere?"

"I've tried, but there are not many jobs around here in the winter, and they won't hire an Indian anyway. Well, I can cut enough wood to keep the fire going and shoot rabbits and ducks and dig clams if there isn't too much ice. But I wish I could earn some money."

The sun was sliding toward the west. "I have to go," Jess said. "Thanks for the stew."

"We are glad to have a guest," Mr. Raven said. "I'll show you a quick way out. Cory will wash the bowls, and you can use her snowshoes."

The snowshoes seemed big and clumsy when they were buckled onto Jess's feet, and he feared he never would be able to walk on them. But when Mr. Raven started out, breaking the trail over the drifts, Jess could easily follow the path he had made. In fifteen minutes they reached the main road, and there Mr. Raven turned back, the extra pair of snowshoes over his shoulder.

When Jess reached home, Tatters was sitting on the doorstep, an apologetic look on her hairy face. The tip of her orange tail wagged faintly. Jess gave her an absentminded pat, muttering, "Good dog," and Tatters was convulsed with joy as she followed him into the house.

Grandmother Manning listened with interest to Jess's story of his visit. "I had no idea you were going onto the Bonnet. The man is right. There is a *No Trespassing* sign, and I can understand why. Hunting rabbits wouldn't do any harm, but the house is lonely and out-of-the-way. Why, someone could practically tear it down and carry it off, and who would know?"

"It's safe enough with the Ravens there. Indians always know if anyone is around."

"I guess that's why the owner hired them," Grandmother said. "The place is so lonely, not many people would like to live there in the winter."

"The house is nice and warm. Mr. Raven has plenty of wood cut."

"I see." Grandmother looked thoughtful. "I wonder if they have any fresh milk or eggs. The little girl looked a bit underfed."

"Oh, they have plenty to eat, rabbit stew and pilot bread, but Cory said they didn't go to the store often." Jess looked uncertain. "Mr. Raven did say something about Mr. Barnes not paying him since he left."

Grandmother pursed her lips. "Could be another reason Mr. Barnes is hiring him. Perhaps he thought he wouldn't have to pay an Indian too often."

"Oh, no. Mr. Raven said it's because he's so busy down in Florida that it probably slipped his mind."

"Easily, I bet," Grandmother said. "I have an idea, Jess. We're going to need wood for next winter, and it's a shame to buy it when this land is growing up to trees. You're too young to cut it alone, and Mr. Raven might be willing to help. We have extra milk and eggs, and there're potatoes, onions, and apples in the cellar. Perhaps we can make a deal with the Ravens to have wood cut in exchange for food."

"That's a great idea," Jess said. Then he asked, "But why don't people like Indians?"

"What makes you think they don't like them?"

"Oh, at the store I hear things. People call Mr. Raven an Injun, and they wonder why Mr. Barnes hired him."

"I don't want you listening to such talk, Jess. White men fought the Indians and took their land. I guess you never feel kindly toward those you rob. Now tomorrow I want you to go over to the Bonnet and invite Cory and her father over here. Tell them we need their help."

The arrangements were made even more easily than they had hoped. Mr. Raven almost smiled at the prospect of a job. He looked at the wood lot with the quick glance of an experienced woodsman. "That's easy. I get four cord in no time. Kids can clean up the brush."

Tatters, barking loudly, ran to the window. "She sees something. What is it, Jess?" Grandmother Manning asked.

"It's some old yellow hound. Wait, it's Doddy Hawthorn and Buck Rogers. What are they doing here?"

Grandmother put down the iron and went to the window. "Hum, they've got guns, and that's Doddy's old hound. They must be rabbit hunting, but why are they coming in here?"

Jess was uneasy. Doddy and Buck were what Grandmother called "worthless." Young, healthy men, they worked a little when they needed money, which wasn't often, because they both lived with their parents. They also hunted, or raided a garden, or stole a few hens on the side.

Buck thumped on the door. "Yes?" Grandmother said, as she opened it.

"Wonder if we could come in and get warm." Buck smiled, showing several bad teeth. "Cold out there hunting. Afraid we'll freeze before we get home."

"Yes, you can come in, but keep that hound

away from our hens," said Grandmother, unable to refuse people in need.

"Yes, ma'am. Sisk-um, you old fool, lie down there." The sad-eyed hound curled up in a corner of the porch, while the men put down their guns and came into the kitchen. They did look cold. Doddy, a big man with a vacant look on his broad face, went over to the stove, took off his mittens, and warmed his hands. Little pools of melting snow from his boots spread over the clean floor.

"Would you like some tea?" Grandmother Manning asked. The water was already boiling.

"Hot tea, now that would be good," Doddy said.

Grandmother found some cups. "Get the milk and sugar, Jess."

Buck Rogers' real name was Tom, but he was always called Buck. He smiled when he saw Jess. "Well, boy, seen any rabbits lately?"

"No, I haven't," Jess said. "Been rabbit hunting?"

"Doddy and I thought we'd give it a try, but we haven't seen much. Old dog found some tracks, but they were going over to the Bonnet."

"You'd best keep away from there." Grandmother poured the tea with a flourish. "That land's posted. You can read that much, Buck."

"Aye, but those signs don't mean anything. Summer complaints always put them up. Old geezer's down South somewhere. He'd never miss a rabbit."

"He's got a caretaker," Jess put in. "An Indian, Mr. Raven."

"Never knew an Injun called mister," Buck said, and Doddy snickered. "Ever seen him, Jess?"

"Sure, I know him. I've been over to the house."

"What's he like? An old man, lazy, sticks around the fire most of the time?"

Grandmother Manning saw the point of his comment. "I'll tell you what he's like. He's big, even for an Indian, but he goes through the woods like a shadow, and he's watching all the time, day and night. You know how Indians are in the woods, crafty as a crow. He's got a shotgun and an axe. He's a crack shot, and I bet he could kill a bear with that axe."

Doddy was beginning to look unhappy.

Grandmother continued. "He's got a kid, too, bright-eyed as a squirrel. I wouldn't go hunting over there, Buck. You'll get a charge of buckshot in your britches."

Buck finished his tea and put the cup aside. "Maybe you're right, Mrs. Manning, but it's a real shame when they'll hire an Injun and let a white man go without a job."

Grandmother banged the cups into the sink. "Maybe they hired him because he'll watch out for the place, and that's more than many a man around here would do."

Jess watched the two men and the yellow hound depart. "You scared them all right," he said.

"I scared Doddy, but I don't know about Buck. That kind's always sneaking about seeing what they can steal. It's just as well to put the fear of God into them from the start."

## CHAPTER FOUR

# Wood Cutting

Spring was here at last. Red and sappy were the baby maples, the willows, and the tiny, gray birches. Pussywillows appeared beside the road, and the swamp turned chocolate brown with alder catkins.

The Ravens appeared early one March morning. It was a mother-of-pearl day, with no sun, only soft gray clouds. The snow settled and cracked, but there was so much of it that in the fields some of the drifts were still waist-deep. The snow was melting, and what remained beside the road was splashed with mud stains. The air had a rich, heavy, moist smell, of mud and rotting leaves and swelling roots.

Mr. Raven carried an axe and saw, and Cory held a large brown paper bag.

"Go and help them, Jess," Grandmother said. "At noon, ask them to come up to the house, and we'll have lunch."

"I think they brought theirs in that bag," Jess pointed out.

"Well, tell them they can eat it here, where it'll be warm. No sense sitting down in the snow to have a cold lunch. I'll have a little extra food, too."

Cutting wood was slow, heavy work. The Indian was a good worker and understood the trees. He knew which were large enough to be worth cutting, in which direction the tree should fall, and how much brush and small trees must be cleared away first. Each tree became a problem—the tiny swamp cedars, the huge, kingly spruces, the flintlike maple, the shaggy-coated yellow birch, even the juniper, which looked as if it were dead. The sound of the axe rang out clearly in the frosty air, and sawdust spilled in cream-colored piles on the trampled snow.

Jess dragged the sticks of wood into a stack, while Cory piled the brush into a great heap in the snow. They were too busy to talk, but when Jess's stomach told him it was noon, he stopped, and said, "Grandma wants to know if you'll come up to the house and eat lunch. It'll be warmer than eating here in the woods."

Mr. Raven put the axe down on a stump, where no one would step on it. "We know how to keep warm, eh, Cory?"

Cory brought out a handful of the wiry, green moss that grows on trees. She had been pulling it off each tree that was cut, so she had a small armful. Placing the moss at the edge of the brush pile, she pulled the pitchy, green branches of fir and spruce over it. With the touch of a match, the moss burned like tinder. Tongues of flame touched the branches, and the fire was roaring. Wisps of sweet woodsmoke drifted above the trees.

Mr. Raven threw a log near the fire for a seat. Cory opened the paper bag and brought out an old agateware coffeepot, blackened by many a campfire. Her father set it on the fire to reheat the coffee. Cory unwrapped the lunch, pilot bread covered with chunks of the dark meat of wild duck.

"You eat with us?" Mr. Raven asked. "It's not much."

"No, thank you." Jess looked regretfully at the wild duck meat. "Grandma's waiting for me, but I'll be back. Maybe she'll let me eat here."

When Jess returned to the house, Grandmother said, "All right. If that's the way they want it. I guess they're happier in the woods than in a strange house. But I've baked potatoes, and I've got a pot of boiled carrots. I'll put some butter on them and get some cream and sugar, and you can take it back to them. That girl needs vegetables."

The cutting was almost finished, and everyone was satisfied. The Mannings would have a supply of wood to keep them warm next winter; the Ravens would have fresh eggs, milk, butter, a sack of potatoes, some onions and carrots, even a couple of jars of sweet cucumber relish.

Later in the afternoon Jess was repairing the door to the hen house when a blue car drove up and stopped. Tatters ran to greet the man who got out, jumping enthusiastically with muddy feet over his clean coat. Jess ran to get the dog as the man, who was middle-aged and rather stout, tried to brush the mud from his coat.

"Good afternoon, Jesse."

"Good afternoon, Reverend Wiley." Jess grabbed Tatters by the collar. "I'm sorry about your coat. Tatters jumps on people, but she's just trying to be friendly."

"Very true. Still, training is always an advantage for a dog or a person. Is your grandmother at home?"

"Oh yes, come in." Jess led the way into the house. He was dying of curiosity to know the reason for the minister's visit. Although the Reverend Wiley called on each family in town at least once a year, it was too early and the dirt road too muddy for him to have made the visit for social purposes alone.

Grandmother Manning made him welcome, sponging the mud from his coat and reprimanding Jess for not watching Tatters' manners.

"It's quite all right, Mrs. Manning," Reverend Wiley said, seating himself in a comfortable chair with a cup of coffee and a plate of cookies before him. "The truth is, I have a problem about which I must seek your help. Do you know the Indian who is living on the Bonnet?"

"Mr. Raven? Yes. In fact, he's cutting wood for me today."

"Splendid! I have received a letter from a Mr. John Barnes, in Florida. I believe he is the owner of the Bonnet."

"Yes, he is," Jess volunteered.

"Capital! Well, Mr. Barnes does not know me personally, but he addressed his letter to the town clergyman. Very ingenious, I thought. He enclosed a letter for Mr. Raven, explaining that he wasn't sure that mail was delivered to the Bonnet or that the man was in the habit of going to the post office. He said he believed that as a man of God I might be entrusted with the delivery of the letter. That was wise. Mr. Barnes must be a fine man."

"Yes," Grandmother agreed, "it was a good idea. It's fortunate you came while Mr. Raven is here. You can take the letter to him, or I'll send Jess with it."

Jess looked out the window. "Cory is coming now. She can take it back."

"He has a little daughter, Cordelia," Grandmother explained. "He calls her Cory. Her mother is dead, I believe."

"I see. The name is a little unusual."

"She was named for the nun who cared for her when she was born," Grandmother Manning said.

Reverend Wiley's face was thoughtful. "That's right. There is a Catholic mission on the reservation."

Cory had come down from the woodlot behind the house, but when she saw the car parked on the road, she stopped and then turned back. Jess ran out of the house to get her.

"Come on, Cory. It's all right. Reverend Wiley won't hurt you."

"No."

"Oh, come on! He's got a letter for your father. You'll have to take it to him."

Curiosity or a sense of duty was stronger than shyness. Cory came on down the path, hands deep in the pockets of her old jacket, and followed Jess into the house.

Grandmother and Mr. Wiley were talking, but they stopped as soon as the children entered. "Cory, dear, this is our minister, the Reverend Mr. Wiley."

Cory stared at the floor. "Hello, Father," she said at last.

Reverend Wiley smiled kindly. "You must not call me Father. Those popish names are not used around here. Mr. Wiley will be fine. I understand you have been living on the Bonnet this winter?"

"Yes, Father."

Reverend Wiley frowned slightly, but his voice was gentle. "I hope you like the town and the people. Your father is very fortunate to have the job."

"Yes, Father."

"Will you please not call me Father?" Reverend Wiley asked with a touch of annoyance. Cory raised her black eyes and gave him a shrewd, searching look.

"Reverend Wiley has a letter for your father," Grandmother spoke up. "Would you take it to him like a good girl?"

"Oh, yes."

"Of course, you'll take it safely and see it's not lost on the way?" The minister looked at Grandmother, not Cory.

"Jess will go with her. It will be all right," Grandmother assured him.

"Fine, here it is," he said, but he handed the letter to Jess, not Cory. "We have a very nice Sunday school, Cordelia, and we would be glad to have you. Any child is welcome."

Cory did not answer, and Jess, sensing uneasiness, said quickly, "Thank you, Reverend Wiley. We better take this letter to Mr. Raven."

"Good-bye, Cordelia," the minister called after them.

They were barely outdoors when Cory snatched the letter from Jess. "That's my father's. Why did he give it to you?"

"Why didn't you talk to him? You acted like you were deaf and dumb. You were scared of him."

"I wasn't scared. Anyway, I had my hand on this, so he couldn't hurt me." Cory pulled the little cross from the neck of her jacket.

"That! How could that protect you?"

"It's been blessed by the Holy Father!"

"That's nothing but superstition!" Jess said.

Cory gave him a hard, black stare, and Jess retreated. "Anyway, your father'll be glad to hear from Mr. Barnes. Maybe he sent some money."

Mr. Raven took the letter and turned it over in his hands, while the children explained how it had been delivered. "Mr. Barnes was good to write. Father was good to bring it."

"He's not called Father. He's called Reverend! Let me read it, Papa," Cory said.

Her father gave her the letter. Cory opened it and began to read, "Dear Mr. Raven, I am sorry to be—" She came to a stop. "I don't know that word."

Jess's suspicions were confirmed. Mr. Raven

couldn't read, but Cory could, except for certain words. "Let me see it," Jess said.

Together they read the letter:

Dear Mr. Raven:

I am sorry to be remiss in writing, but I have been extremely busy. You have no idea how commercial and artificial life is in other parts of the country. I look forward to spending the summer in beautiful, unspoiled Maine. I have purchased a boat in Summerport, and in April the boatyard will bring it to the Bonnet. Could you have a mooring ready? I will be at the Bonnet myself by late April.

Oh yes, in regard to your salary, I think it will be best to wait until I arrive and make full payment then.

Yours truly,
John Barnes

Cory rolled up the letter in her hand and looked up at her father. "I thought he'd send us some money, Papa, so we could go to the store. We haven't had any bread for a long time."

Jess was embarrassed, for he knew Grandmother could not loan them any money. "Maybe the store at Summerport would let you buy some things on credit. You could tell them Mr. Barnes is going to pay you when he comes," he suggested.

Mr. Raven took the letter from Cory and put it in his pocket. "No, Jess, that would be like begging. There are still rabbits on the Bonnet, and we can hold out until Mr. Barnes comes. Cory, we'll go clamming tomorrow. Perhaps we can sell some clams in Summerport, and then we can buy some more crackers and bread."

## CHAPTER FIVE

# The Owner Arrives

The snow was gone at last. Only in the deep woods little patches of it remained. Alder catkins, covered with pollen, made a golden haze against the silver pussywillows, and the roadside brooks were noisy. Waves of birds passed over the land, and there was constant twittering from every bush. High overhead, a fish hawk screamed monotonously.

Jess was trudging along the muddy road to

the Bonnet, carrying a jug of fresh milk. Since the wood cutting had ended, there had been little communication between the families, but Grandmother worried about Cory. "That child should have fresh milk. I don't suppose they'd ask for it, that would be too much like charity, but there's no harm in taking them a gift. I do hope that wise, God-fearing Mr. Barnes will arrive soon with some money."

Tatters came, too, taking side trips through the woods, sniffing around every windfall for invisible rabbits. There was no sign of people. The house came into sight—dark, hostile, forbidding. Jess thought, why would Mr. Barnes want to live in such a lonely, inhospitable place? But Mr. Barnes had answered that question. He had written how artificial and commercial his surroundings had become. Probably he wanted a place that was peaceful and quiet. In a few weeks the Bonnet would be beautiful.

Jess turned into a driveway leading to the

wing of the house that the Ravens used as a home. Tatters trotted gaily ahead, her tail up like a banner. Suddenly out of the dead ferns by the road rose a huge black beast. At least, it looked huge, for every hair on the animal stood upright. It was Jet. His back was arched like a bridge, his tail like a bottle brush. His ears were laid back, and white fangs showed as he spat.

Tatters stopped, and without hesitation the cat attacked. One, two, three raps with the steellike claws. The first blow landed on Tatters' hairy paw, the second on her furry shoulder, the third on her tender, chocolate nose. Howling with pain and terror, the dog flew up the driveway, and, finding the door open, took refuge in the kitchen.

"Cut that out, Jet!" the boy cried. The cat edged around him, crab fashion, a contemptuous look in his green eyes. Then he padded on after the dog. When Jess reached the entrance to the house, Tatters was besieged under the kitchen table. Jet prowled in front of the door, muttering curses.

Jess looked around for some distraction. He grabbed a tin plate from under a tree, pulled the stopper out of the jug, and poured some milk into the plate. "Here, Jet. Here, nice pussy."

Jet paused, sniffed, straightened the arch in his back, and sampled the milk daintily. As Jess was about to rescue Tatters, Cory appeared. She took in the scene in a glance and began to giggle. "Jet was ready for her that time. He wasn't going to be chased up a tree."

"He scratched Tatters' nose. I thought he was going to kill her."

"Why are you here?" Cory asked, with a sudden lack of friendliness.

"Grandma sent over this jug of milk."

"Oh, good. Papa will give you some maple syrup." Cory took the jug into the kitchen. The room was very warm, for a hot fire was going in the stove, and Cory added more wood to the blaze. A large kettle occupied half of the stove, and the air was filled with the faint fragrance of maple.

"Real maple syrup! Can I help?" Jess asked.

"Sure, we found a lot of sugar maples down on the point, but it's a long way to carry the sap. Papa sent me back to put more wood in the stove. We've got to keep the sap boiling." Cory put the milk in the cool back room. "Come along," she said.

Tatters crept out from under the table, keeping well in advance of the children. Jet had finished the milk, and he pattered along with Cory, paying no attention to the dog. The path led along a ridge to a hill overlooking Backside Cove. Mr. Raven, holding an auger in his hand, was inspecting one of the old, large, gray maples.

"Papa, Jess brought us some milk. He's going to help us."

"Good." Mr. Raven picked up a pail, went over to a tree, and with the auger bored a hole

into the trunk. Then he drove a wooden spout into the hole, and on the end of the spout he hung a tin bucket. The pail hanging on a nearby tree was nearly full of what looked like clear rainwater. Mr. Raven emptied its contents into a large pail. "Sap runs good. Cold nights, warm days. That's what makes sap run."

For the first time Jess looked down into Backside Cove. "Oh, Mr. Barnes's boat's here."

"Yes, it came last week. Papa dumped an old car engine overboard for a mooring."

The boat was large, with an inboard motor, but hardly a yacht. It had been painted gray, but now the paint was so weathered that the boat looked old and shabby. There was a cabin to protect the cockpit, but it was a ramshackle affair. Some of the boards were falling off, and the windshield was cracked. Jess had expected Mr. Barnes to own quite a different sort of boat.

"It's awfully low in the water," Jess said.

"Yes, I haven't pumped it out today."

"Papa has to pump it out every day," Cory said. "It leaks so badly, it would sink if he didn't."

"Has anyone been out in it yet?"

Mr. Raven shrugged. "The engine doesn't work."

"They towed it over from Summerport," Cory explained. "Mr. Barnes is going to have a lot of work done on it. He's going on a cruise at the end of the summer. I guess he bought it so he could fix it the way he wants it."

They worked the rest of the afternoon, lugging pails of sap up to the house and storing it in tubs to await boiling. Tatters chased squirrels, and Jet stalked the fat fox sparrows that were scratching in the leaves under the maple trees, but there wasn't any more trouble between them. Jess went home with a small bottle of real maple syrup and with plenty of news to tell Grandmother.

"The boat is there now. Mr. Barnes is going on a cruise, but he's going to have a lot of work done on it first."

"It'll be a busy season there," Grandmother agreed.

One day in late April a gray station wagon with out-of-state plates stopped in front of the Manning house, and a man got out. Jess was splitting wood by the barn. "Tatters! Behave yourself!" he shouted, for the dog was charging happily with muddy feet toward the visitor. The man was middle-aged, slender, and good-looking, his tanned skin making him appear very fit and healthy.

"Hello, son. I'm Mr. Barnes, owner of the Bonnet. I wonder if it's possible to drive down there. As I recall, the road is not in very good condition this time of year."

"No, sir, you couldn't drive there now. The frost is just coming out, and you'd drop right through the mud."

"I was afraid so, but there are things I must attend to. Do you ever see the caretaker?"

"Oh yes. We like Mr. Raven. He cut some wood for us this winter. Did you know the boat is there? Mr. Raven has a mooring for it."

"Good!" The man had an engaging smile. "That's one reason I came early. I bought the boat at a low price, and it needs much work done on it to get it ready for the cruise."

Grandmother Manning had observed the visitor, and now she came to the door. Mr. Barnes removed his hat and introduced himself. "I was asking your boy the condition of the road down to the Bonnet."

"You'll never make it, not in a car anyway."

"But I'm staying several weeks to arrange for work to be done on the boat. Then I have to leave on a short trip. I'll need to bring in groceries and other things as well."

"Why don't you drive back to Summerport and have the man at the boatyard take you across the cove? You could leave your car in

Summerport. It doesn't take too long to get across the cove, and the house isn't far from the beach. Mr. Raven could help you carry up your groceries."

"Yes," Jess put in, "and they have an old skiff we found. You can row across to Summerport whenever you want to."

"A good idea. I shall have to learn the primitive life if I'm going on a cruise. Thank you for your help. I hope you'll visit me at the Bonnet." Turning to Jess, he went on, "Perhaps I can find a job there for you this summer."

When he had driven away, Jess said, "Mr. Barnes seems awfully nice, doesn't he Grandma?"

"Yes, and I'm glad to see some interest in the place at last."

"Wouldn't it be wonderful if I could get a job? Maybe I could earn enough to buy my winter clothes."

"That would be a good idea," his grandmother agreed. "I hope Mr. Barnes remembers to pay those Indians. He was kind to hire them, but it was hardly kind to let them go all winter without pay."

"Oh, now that he's here, he'll pay them, I'm sure," Jess assured her.

## CHAPTER SIX

# A Job

The earth was drying out fast, becoming soft and crumbly. In a few weeks it would be ready for planting. Robins sang every night until sundown. The hens were outdoors hunting for bugs in the new earth, and the speckled cow looked longingly out the barn window, but it was too damp for her to be out.

"You must check over that fence before we put Bossy out," Grandmother said, "and the lawn must be raked. Soon it'll be time to mow it." Green blades of grass already were appearing.

"I'll do it tomorrow. Today I want to see Mr. Barnes about the job he mentioned."

"All right."

It was a quick walk in late April over a road that had taken so long to travel on snowshoes that winter. The station wagon was parked in front of the great house, but there was no sign of activity. The windows still glared, hostile and remote.

Jess had left Tatters at home, for he wasn't sure if Mr. Barnes liked animals, but when he turned onto the path leading to the servants' quarters, he saw that Jet was still there. The black cat was napping in the sun, and he looked up at Jess with a cold, disapproving eye.

The door to the kitchen was open, but no one was there. The fire was out in the big stove, and there was no sign of maple sap. On the floor were several orange crates filled with canned goods and groceries. Someone had been to the store.

Jess followed the path toward the grove of maples, Jet pattering along behind him. A hammer was pounding, and Jess turned in that direction. The cove was very still, the water a pale, washed-out blue, and the shabby boat swung idly at its mooring. The Ravens were busy in a little field near the beach. The old skiff had been hauled up, and they were painting it.

"Hello," Jess called.

"Hi," Cory answered. Her father glanced up, but said nothing.

"It looks super," Jess said. "Where did you get the paint?" The color was bright red, one Jess never had seen used on a boat before.

"Mr. Barnes gave it to us."

"I see you've got some groceries. You must have been to the store."

"Aye," Mr. Raven said, continuing the work.

"Where's Mr. Barnes?"

"He's resting," Cory said. "He rests every afternoon."

Jess sensed a disenchantment on the part of the Ravens. "I thought there'd be all sorts of work going on here. I was hoping to get a job. No one has touched the boat yet, and I thought he was going on a cruise."

"Yes, he's going a long ways off. He's selling the place here." Mr. Raven nodded toward the house.

"Selling it!" Jess was shocked. "But I thought he was going to spend his summers here."

"He's bought a house in Florida," Cory said. "He wants to cruise down there."

"Then I guess I won't get a job. I thought there was going to be a lot of work to do."

"Ask him," Mr. Raven said. "Already he's hired two men to fix up the boat."

A flicker called from the woods, and then Jet, who had been sniffing around a field mouse's hole, stopped suddenly and glared in the direction of the house. Mr. Barnes appeared on the banking. His strong, athletic build made him look young, but his face showed that he was older than he had first seemed.

"Hi, Jess," he called, friendly enough. "Come to look at the work our Indian friends are doing?"

The black cat disappeared into the bushes. Jess kicked his toe into the soft moss, and said, "I was wondering if I could get a job here this summer."

"Why not? I can use a good, steady worker like you."

"I thought there wouldn't be much work now, if you're going to sell the place." Jess was surprised at how quickly the offer had been accepted. After all, Mr. Barnes hardly knew him. How did he know he was a "good, steady worker"?

"Oh, our Indian friends have been talking!" Mr. Barnes said. "Well, there'll be plenty to do. We want the place to look attractive when it's up for sale, and there will be a great deal of work to do before the boat is seaworthy. I've already hired two young men from Summerport to repair it. Perhaps you know them, Mr. Hawthorn and Mr. Rogers."

Jess gulped. "Yes, I know them." He was aware that Mr. Barnes was watching him closely, but he didn't dare to say more. How can you tell a decent stranger that he couldn't have picked a lazier pair to do the work?

"Good, we shall all get along fine. You come over the first of May, and we'll get you started. We'll talk wages then. I plan to be away for a while, and I want everything moving here before I leave."

But that afternoon when Jess told his grandmother he had a job on the Bonnet, starting May first, she didn't seem pleased. "The garden will have to be planted in May."

"It'll only take a few days to plant the garden, and it's too early to do any weeding. I could be working and earning money."

"There's plenty of work to be done here, even if there isn't any money in it. That pasture fence must be repaired, and we should have a yard built for the hens before they dig up the garden."

"I'll never get a chance to earn any money," Jess complained. "When Mr. Barnes stopped here a few days ago and spoke of a job, you didn't say anything against it."

"The truth is, things have changed," his grandmother said. "I don't want you working with men like Buck or Doddy. Mr. Barnes must be a fool or very ill-advised to hire them. They're lazy, incompetent, and will steal everything on the place. I don't want you mixed up in such a business."

It was a warm, bright day, almost like summer, and in the garden by the house four little crocuses bared their hearts to the sun. The first of the bees were buzzing around them, hunting for pollen. Jess was mending the wire of the cow pasture, and Tatters had gone off to hunt meadow mice in the old field when the gray station wagon stopped, and Mr. Barnes got out.

"Hard at work? This is a fine farm you have," he said.

Jess was pleased. Few people call a place

with one cow and a dozen hens a farm. "Well, it's pretty small. Just Grandmother and I run it."

"But it's very neat and well cared for, and I like the way you work. Speaking of work, I thought you'd be over to the Bonnet by this time."

"I've decided not to come. Grandmother thinks there's enough to do here."

"Doesn't she realize you could be earning a little money?"

"I don't know." Jess twisted the wire in his fingers. He dared not mention the real reason why Grandmother wouldn't let him work at the Bonnet.

"Is your grandmother at home? Perhaps I could speak with her. You see, I was going to offer you a dollar and a half an hour. That's pretty good money for a twelve year old."

"I'm thirteen," Jess corrected, but he opened his eyes wide. He never had expected to be paid so well. "Grandmother's in the kitchen.

Maybe you could talk her into letting me."

"Well, I can try."

Grandmother was as impressed as Jess by the wage offer. "It's really very good of you, sir. The trouble is, I'd rather not have Jess working with the workmen you've hired."

"You mean the Indian family?"

"Of course not. Mr. Raven is a fine man, and I've become very fond of the little girl. I wish I saw her more often. But Buck and Doddy, the men who will be working on the boat, are a rough crew."

"I see." Mr. Barnes looked thoughtful. "Of course, I am a newcomer, and I may have made a mistake, but as these men were the only ones in town without work, I decided to hire them. Often when men get a bad name, they are unable to find work, even after they have changed. When I'm away, I shall have an overseer in charge, and if he finds Mr. Hawthorn and Mr. Rogers are not working out well, he'll let them go.

"You know," he went on, "I talked with Reverend Wiley, to thank him for his kindness in delivering the letter. I spoke of my plans to hire Mr. Hawthorn and Mr. Rogers, and he mentioned the same difficulty that you have. Then I pointed out to him that it really would be a mercy to give these men a chance, as I did the Indian family. He agreed the idea was splendid."

"Well, there is truth in what you say," Grandmother Manning agreed. "I'll let Jess work there for a while if he wishes."

"That's fine. Jess is a fine, intelligent boy, the kind I like to help."

## CHAPTER SEVEN

# Work on the Bonnet

Jess, his lunch bucket under his arm, was going to work, to the first real paying job in his life. He had left Tatters at home. The new overseer at the Bonnet might not want a dog around the place, so she had been chained outside the barn. Her heartbroken cries of "Oh! Oh! Oh! Oh!" followed Jess all the way to the Bonnet road. Tatters never barked or howled as most dogs do when they are unhappy; she yodeled. Jess hardened his heart, and soon he was out of hearing.

Peace lay over the lonely road. The poplar trees wore soft, green halos, and the swamp maples in full bloom had become burning bushes. Over the road where maple blossoms had fallen lay a bright crimson froth.

There were changes at the house, too. For the first time the front door was open, and some of the windows had curtains to veil their cold, blank stare. The big, gray station wagon had gone, and in its place a little black Volkswagen stood in the driveway.

Jess went to the servants' wing, where the Ravens lived, but there was no sign of life. Even the cat had vanished. Then he went to the front door, called, and waited. There was no answer, but he could hear a radio playing somewhere in the house. Jess could see into the hallway, which was almost as large as his grandmother's whole house, and up the great, arching stairway. He called again, and still there was no answer. Then a door in the hallway opened, apparently by chance, and a girl carrying a dust mop in her hand appeared.

"Jess Manning! What are you doing here?"

"Kathy May!" He had not expected to see Kathy May Turner of Summerport at the Bonnet. "Are you working here, too?"

Kathy May went to the door and shook the mop. "Aye, doing a little mopping up. The overseer hired me to clean up the place and do a little cooking. Wait, I'll call him and tell him you're here."

As Jess waited, he thought, Hiring people from Summerport was a good idea, but why did Mr. Barnes always choose the poorest workers? Kathy May was not well known for her cooking or cleaning abilities.

The man who came out smoking a cigarette was not the sort of overseer Jess had expected. Mr. Barnes had spoken of a man of great energy and experience, who had been his friend for a long time. This man was much younger than Mr. Barnes; he even seemed

younger than Buck Rogers. He was blond and quite handsome.

"Hello, kid. What's your name?"

"Jesse Manning, sir. Mr. Barnes told me I could have a job here."

"I'm Fred Rockwell. You're to look after the lawns. Well, you can get to work."

"What do you want me to do? I've never had a job before," he added, fearing that Mr. Rockwell would think him stupid.

"Come along. I'll show you. Be back in a minute, Kathy May." They went out to the driveway, and Mr. Rockwell stopped to survey the lawn, as if a little uncertain himself as to what should be done. "John wants only the front yard cut. Let the people who buy it clean up the back."

Jess knew his grandmother would disapprove of such a remark, but he did not object. "It's got to be raked before it's mowed," he said, looking at the tangle of old dead grass through which new growth was showing.

Many rocks and cans also were scattered about.

"Yes, you're right, but I don't know where they keep the tools." For an overseer he seemed oddly incompetent.

"Where's Mr. Raven? He might know."

"The Injun? Off sulking somewhere. You know, the noble red man doesn't like to have a paleface giving him orders."

"I like the Ravens."

"Sure, you can't help liking them. But Indians are dumb and lazy, and they never make good workers."

Jess thought of the wood Mr. Raven had cut last winter, but he held his tongue. He didn't want to quarrel with the overseer.

In a shed behind the house they unearthed a bamboo rake with several teeth missing, a wheelbarrow in need of oil, and a very rusty hand lawn mower.

"You'll have to make them do," Mr. Rockwell said. "Rake up the worst of the mess on the front lawn today. Don't be fussy. The place is going to be sold anyway. Then you can come back and mow some other day. Make the job last as long as possible. Now I've got some things to attend to in the house."

Jess took the old wheelbarrow and the battered rake and went to work on the lawn. "Oh boy!" he said to himself, "talk about being a good worker. I wonder when Mr. Rockwell does any work."

The job went smoothly. Jess, who had learned to work from his grandmother, had it finished by noon. He took his lunch bucket and went around to the servants' wing to eat in the shade of the pines. He had just unwrapped the ham sandwich when a small, black animal slipped out of the bushes. "Meow," said Jet.

Jess broke off part of the sandwich and handed it to the cat, who ate it daintily. "Where are the rest of them?" he asked.

"Right here." Cory's approach had been as silent as Jet's.

"Want a sandwich?" Jess said. "Where've you been all morning?"

Cory took the sandwich quickly. "Over to Sculpin Cove digging clams. Papa's out in the shed now looking at the lawn mower."

"It needs looking at all right," Jess agreed.

Mr. Raven had pushed the mower out into the sun and was rubbing the rust from its dull blade.

"Bad," he said, shaking his head.

"Mr. Rockwell says I've got to use it. There isn't any other. He says it doesn't matter how the lawn looks."

"Mr. Rockwell says it doesn't matter how anything looks."

"You don't like him?"

Mr. Raven shrugged, but Cory said, "Why is Mr. Barnes so stupid, Jess? Mr. Rockwell doesn't do any work, that girl doesn't do any work, those two men down on the shore aren't doing any work, yet Mr. Barnes pays them."

"Jess is the best worker in the bunch," her father said.

"I don't know." Jess felt there was something about the situation that he didn't understand. "When Mr. Barnes comes back next month, he'll straighten things out. How're Buck and Doddy getting along on the boat?"

Mr. Raven went into the shed and returned with an old wrench and a can of oil. "Go look at them."

Jess put away his lunch bucket, and then with Cory he started for the shore. Jet pattered along behind them. Mr. Raven remained behind, still working on the mower.

"We'll have to be careful with Jet," Cory said. "They throw rocks at him. Do you know, Mr. Rockwell even tried to run over him? Papa is talking about going back to the reservation."

"Do you want to go?" Jess asked.

"No, I like it here. There're going to be berries to pick this summer, and now that we have the skiff we can go fishing. But Papa doesn't like Mr. Rockwell or Mr. Hawthorn, and they don't like us."

"Wait until Mr. Barnes comes. Things will be different then," Jess promised, but in his heart he wondered.

The boat was ashore, lying on its side on the coarse beach gravel. The Ravens' bright red skiff also was pulled up on land. A small stack of new lumber, plywood, and buckets of paint were scattered about the field that bordered the beach. Buck and Doddy were working on the boat, shoving caulking into the seams between the planks. Although they kept the tools in their hands, much of the time they stood talking.

Jet disappeared, as if by magic, and the children walked onto the beach. Although Jess didn't know much about boats, even he could see that very little had been accomplished.

"Hi, there," Buck called, as the children approached. "How's my little papoose today?"

The words were friendly, but Cory stared at him coldly.

"Didn't she tell you she's my little Injun sweetheart?" Buck smiled and hummed a few bars of *Redwing,* very much out of tune.

Embarrassed, Jess turned the conversation to their job. "When are you going to get the boat off?"

"Next month maybe, after Mr. Barnes gets here. We're coming along fine. Lots to do, though." He put his tools down on the beach and took out a package of cigarettes, while Doddy leaned against the boat, watching him.

"May as well take a rest. Want one, Jess?" he asked, offering a cigarette.

"No, thanks."

"Just as well. It's a dirty habit. Wish I could get a word out of that cute little Injun. Think that old cat got her tongue?"

"What are you going to do with all that lumber in the field?" Jess asked, keeping the conversation on course.

"Well, we're going to build a big cabin on the boat, so he can live aboard. But first we've got to get it watertight and painted. It takes a long time, you know, to do a decent job."

That afternoon Jess returned home with a pail of clams, a gift from the Ravens, and he told Grandmother all the things that had happened at the Bonnet and of Cory's remark that they might return to the reservation. "I'll be sorry if they go," he added. "I'll miss them like anything."

"Mr. Raven has had the place to himself this winter," Grandmother said. "He probably resents having the workmen around, but he'll get over that."

"But, Grandmother, they aren't doing much of anything there. The boat looks terrible."

"It will as long as Buck and Doddy work on it," she replied.

"I thought the overseer, Mr. Rockwell, was going to see that everyone was doing his job, but he spends all his time just loafing."

"That figures," Grandmother said.

"The Ravens think Mr. Barnes is stupid to let things go on this way."

"I don't think he's stupid, but he is busy. A man like that must have a great deal on his mind. I suppose the Bonnet must be very small apples to him. Since there doesn't seem to be any great rush on things over at the Bonnet, I think it's time we got the garden planted. We'll start tomorrow."

# CHAPTER EIGHT

# Planting the Garden

On the edge of the woods the miracle of the leaves had begun. Fiddleheads, feathery soft, uncurled where once only dead fronds had been. The new leaves of the wild cherry were russet; those of the wild pear were dun-colored. Little mountain maple leaves were sticky with red varnish. Loveliest of all were the beech leaves, bursting their pale pink wrapping, exquisite as butterfly wings of watered, green silk.

In the fields there were clouds of blue violets and little everlastings; in the woods were yards of tiny, white violets and the fluffy stars of the goldthread. Purple trilliums that had popped up in one night were in flower.

For three days Jess and Grandmother worked on the garden. It already had been plowed and harrowed. The silky, brown loam was ready to be seeded. Jess brought out the rake and hoe, and Grandmother filled the big basket with seed packages and the stakes to mark the rows.

Jess made shallow furrows for the little seeds, deeper ones for the beans and corn, and very deep ones for the potatoes. Grandmother dropped the seeds in them carefully and precisely. Then they both covered the seeds with earth as tenderly as if they were living things, which, of course, they were. All through the planting, two grackles swayed high up in the top of the maple, their liquid calls bubbling like drops of rain.

"Can I go back to work at the Bonnet?"

Jess asked several days after they had finished working on the garden. "I'm supposed to mow the lawn."

"You may as well. We can certainly use the money. It's June now, and Mr. Barnes should come any time."

Not much had changed on the Bonnet, but the road was now firm and dry. Someone obviously had attempted to mow the lawn, for the grass had a ragged half-cut look.

"I had to stay home and plant the garden," Jess explained to Mr. Rockwell. "Can I start work today?"

"Sure, go ahead," the overseer answered. "The Injun got the mower working and did a little mowing himself, but you can't depend on him. Injuns aren't much interested in working, you know."

The rust and old grass had been cleaned from the lawn mower, and the wheels had been oiled, so that it could be moved at least, although the dull blades tore the grass instead of cutting it. Jess worked hard, and the lawn did look better, even though a first-class job was impossible until the mower was sharpened. Tired and thirsty, he opened his lunch pail to get the bottle of pop Grandmother had packed. He was drinking it when the overseer appeared.

"You've been here a couple of hours, kid," he said, looking at his watch. "Better quit before you get too tired. You can come back tomorrow."

"I didn't do a good job. The blade's so dull that it doesn't cut right."

"Well, perhaps it can be sharpened. John's coming back tomorrow. He can decide."

"I wonder, could I bring my dog when I come again? Tatters hates to stay home."

"Sure. It won't bother me any."

Jess thought of what Cory had said of Mr. Rockwell's attempt to run over Jet. She must have been mistaken. Cats are always dodging in front of cars. "Do you mind if I go down and see how the boat's coming along?" Jess asked.

"No, go ahead."

Jess had not seen any sign of the Ravens all day, but when he started down the path to the shore he wasn't surprised to hear a soft, "Preow." Jet stepped out of the bushes with Cory close behind him.

"I heard you working on the lawn, and I hoped you'd come down here."

"You're never up around the house anymore."

"They don't want Indians around." Then Cory said, "Papa and I are going to have a picnic down at Sculpin Cove tonight. Can you come, Jess?"

"If Grandma will let me."

"Of course, you may go," his grandmother said, when Jess asked her later in the day. "I'll give you a bag of cookies to take with you. You'd better take Tatters, too. She's grieving her heart out."

The sun was setting when they arrived at the Bonnet, bypassing the great house and following the little path past Backside Cove and out onto the point. Wild geese called, and three of them, stragglers, passed over northward, flying very high. Behind them, Jupiter shone clearly, looking terribly distant, as brilliant stars in the early evening do.

Sculpin Cove was only a notch in the cliffs, a small, sandy beach fenced in by gray, slate rocks. The Ravens had made a tiny fire, no more than a glow in the soft darkness. At sundown the robins had been complaining loudly, but now they were quiet. From the old abandoned fields, the woodcock began calling, a loud monotonous squawk. A few frogs were croaking in the swamp. Soon it echoed with them, like women chattering at a sewing circle.

Tatters was shy in the night, and she kept close to Jess. The smoke drifted into the darkness, and the smell of boiling shellfish came from the fire. As Jess sat there, he became

aware of the black cat beside Cory, his eyes glowing in the firelight. He looked silently at Tatters, who crept up, looking very humble.

"Are you steaming clams?" Jess asked.

"Mussels." Cory slipped the cover off the kettle and lifted out the shellfish with an old, steel, pronged fork.

"Are they good to eat?"

"They're good," Mr. Raven said. "Plenty of them around here. White people waste food."

"No one around here will eat them," Cory said, as she drained the water from the kettle. "Mr. Rogers and Mr. Hawthorn say they're poison."

The mussels smelled delicious. Tatters edged over to Cory, a hopeful look in her hungry eyes. Jet rubbed against his mistress, quite sure of his reward.

Cory dumped the shellfish out onto a clean board. After opening them like steamed clams,

Jess tasted them cautiously. The orange flesh was as sweet as oysters.

"This may be our last picnic before we go back to the reservation," Cory said suddenly.

"But why?" Jess asked.

"Well, there's no church, and I miss the good Sisters."

"There *is* a church. You could go with us. Reverend Wiley invited you."

"He just said that. He didn't really want me. The only kind people here are you and your grandmother and Mr. Barnes."

"We were glad to have a job off the reservation, and we had a good winter," Mr. Raven said. "Now there are bad people around. Mr. Hawthorn and Mr. Rogers steal small things —nails and boards. Mr. Rockwell sees nothing. If they accuse us of stealing these things, everyone will believe them."

"Mr. Barnes won't," Jess said. "He knew from the start that Buck and Doddy weren't very honest, but he gave them a chance. Reverend Wiley knows, too."

"They will not take an Indian's word against a white man's," Mr. Raven stated.

"That's not true. Anyone who knew you would believe you. The trouble is, Grandma and Mr. Barnes and I are the only ones who know you. If other people saw you as much as we have, they'd like you, too. Why don't you go out to the store more often or let Cory go to church with us?"

Cory's eyes had a dark, brooding look. Her father said, "No, Jess. It is best we keep to ourselves or go away before trouble comes. There will be trouble. That I know."

As Jess went home through the warm summer night, he thought deeply about Mr. Raven's words, and he felt uneasy about what might happen. Of course, there was bound to be trouble with men like Doddy and Buck doing the work, and an incompetent like Fred Rockwell in charge. Then Jess comforted himself with the thought that Mr. Barnes would return tomorrow and would see at once how much material and time had been wasted, and how little work had been done. He would straighten things out, for sure.

"Just the same," Jess said to Tatters, "we won't say anything to Grandma. If she gets the idea something is wrong, she won't let us work there anymore."

# CHAPTER NINE

# A Quarrel

The horse chestnut tree that grew by the Manning house held its blossoms up like great white candles. A sweet breath drifted in from the apple orchard. The morning was cool, unbelievably lovely, the sea like glass, the hills blurred by haze. The heat increased with the rising sun, and there was not a breath of wind.

Jess and Tatters went to work early. There was so much to do at the Bonnet, and he had accomplished so little that Jess was discouraged. The tools were old and rusty, and no matter how hard he tried, he couldn't do a good job with them. The hedges were a thicket, and weeds were starting to grow in the driveway.

Mr. Rockwell was usually invisible, but this morning he was waiting by the door. "Hey, kid, bring that wheelbarrow around here, and take this load of junk down to the beach and dump it. The boss is coming today, and we've got to smarten the place up a bit."

Kathy May was sweeping the rooms, making the dust fly for the first time. Fred Rockwell carried out a big box filled with tin cans and bottles.

"We shouldn't dump those on the beach," Jess said.

"Why not? The tide will carry them out."

Jess said nothing, but he remembered his grandmother's complaint about the broken bottles and rusty cans that cut the feet of children on the bathing beach. There was a deep gully at the head of the field by the cove. He would dump them there.

He almost had reached the gully when the cat, Jet, came dashing past him, hair up, tail kiting out behind him. "What's wrong, Jet?" he called, but the cat did not stop. Tatters, running ahead with her ears up, started barking. Then Jess heard loud voices. Doddy and Buck often shouted at one another when they were working, but these shouts were angry, and one of the voices was Mr. Raven's.

Jess dropped the wheelbarrow and dashed after the dog. Mr. Raven stood over the red skiff at the water's edge, an axe in his hand. A little way up the beach, facing him, were Buck and Doddy, who was holding a two-by-four like a club in his hand. Cory stood silently by the alders at the edge of the field.

"Go ahead, hit him, Doddy," Buck called.

"White thief! You'll get axe through head," the Indian growled.

Tatters ran gaily down onto the beach, and they stared at her. "Jess!" Cory cried. "They're going to steal our boat. Tell Mr. Rockwell!"

Jess turned and ran as fast as he could back up the path to the house. He was panting when he reached the yard. There, beside the Volkswagen was the gray station wagon with the Florida license plates. Mr. Barnes had arrived!

"Mr. Barnes! Mr. Barnes!" he shouted, tearing into the house. "Quick! Mr. Raven and Buck and Doddy, they're going to have a fight. They'll kill each other!"

Mr. Barnes appeared instantly, and he reacted to Jess's confused story much more quickly than Mr. Rockwell. A small, thin, sandy-haired man, whom Jess did not recognize, joined them, but Jess paid little attention to him. Mr. Barnes said, "Come on, Greg. We've got to get down there before the darn fools kill themselves."

The three men hurried down the path while Jess gave a clearer account of what had occurred. "Hard to tell who is the dumber, the Indian or the natives," Mr. Barnes said. Jess did not think of it then, but later he remembered the contempt in the man's voice.

The situation on the beach had changed with the knowledge that Jess had gone for help. The Ravens were working around the skiff, unloading some buckets of clams, while Doddy and Buck were restacking some of the lumber on the edge of the field. Even Tatters was busy, rolling in the body of a dead crab that she had discovered on the shoreline.

Mr. Barnes did not waste words. "What's wrong here?" Jess was aware of a change in the man's mood. He seemed more businesslike, less inclined to use flattering words.

"Well now," Buck said with a whine, "if we're going to get that yacht in the water, we'll need a skiff to get it out there. I asked that brown heathen if we could use his, and he said no."

Mr. Raven banged down the bucket of clams. "He asked for nothing! He takes, like all his people."

"They were going to take our skiff and pull lobster traps," Cory cried. "Then people would blame us for stealing lobsters."

Mr. Barnes ignored Cory, but he spoke firmly to Buck. "That skiff belongs to the Indians and you remember that, Rogers. I've brought a boat with me to help with the work on the yacht, but it is possible we'll also need the skiff. Would you be willing to rent it, Mr. Raven?"

"You ask. That's different. I'm proud to loan anything to a friend. To take without asking is wrong."

The newcomer, Greg, showed no interest in the quarrel. He had walked down to the boat and was examining it carefully, not with curiosity, but with an air of inspection. Buck became uneasy, perhaps because he realized that inspection was the last thing his work could stand. He joined the man and began explaining the troubles in repairing an old boat, why this plank was a little crooked or another poorly nailed.

The stranger listened in silence. Then he said, "We've brought a boat on top of the station wagon. I want the two of you to carry it down here. We're going to put this boat in water on the next high tide. The work will be finished when it is afloat."

Mr. Barnes looked at him with admiration. "This is Greg Martin, a friend of mine. He's going on the cruise with me. He's a scuba diver, too, you know, and he's brought his equipment with him."

Jess was thrilled. "You mean he's one of those fellows who swims around with a tank of air on his back and wears things like frogs' feet?"

Mr. Barnes laughed. "Yes, and when we get the boat running, we're going to have a wonderful time exploring all the shores and islands. Can you swim, Jess?"

"Oh, no. The water's too cold."

"With a wet suit you don't mind the cold. Some people even swim when it's freezing," Mr. Barnes pointed out.

"None of the folks around here can swim," Buck said. "My old man told me always to plan to stay in the boat, not to go fooling around outside in the water."

Mr. Barnes laughed again, and a sense of harmony was restored. "All right, men," Greg Martin said, "we'll go up to the house and bring that boat down."

He started off, followed by Doddy and Buck. Jess picked up the wheelbarrow, whistled to Tatters, and went along with the men. Only the Indians remained on the beach.

The summer drought was upon them. Clover wilted, and the hairy leaves of the hawkweed turned in at the edges. When Jess hoed the garden, the dust rose in little puffs. High in a maple tree, a vireo called monotonously, hour after hour, emphasizing the heat.

Night brought relief with its coolness, but it also brought swarms of mosquitoes.

"Better not do any more hoeing," Grandmother said. "It's only drying out the earth. We'll have to wait until it rains."

Jess knew he should be worried about the garden, but he wasn't. There were too many other things on his mind. He was glad that the dry weather made much farming impossible, for he had a good excuse to return to the Bonnet.

"I don't see how their lawn can need mowing in this dry weather," Grandmother complained. "Ours doesn't."

"Maybe I can help Mr. Martin with the boat."

"I should think with six men working on the place, they wouldn't need a boy."

"Oh, they need me."

"When will you be getting your pay?" Grandmother said.

"Mr. Barnes is going to pay me in a lump

sum at the end of the summer," Jess answered.

Many things were happening on the Bonnet that Jess didn't understand, but he didn't discuss them with Grandmother. Mr. Barnes seemed interested only in the *Sea Lark,* which was natural, Jess supposed, since he would be leaving the Bonnet soon, and the *Sea Lark* would be his home. Jess was fascinated by the equipment—the black wet suit with the white stripe down its side, the flippers, the helmet and goggles, and the air tanks. He was disappointed that Greg Martin gave him so little attention. Mr. Martin was a hard worker and an efficient organizer. Already Doddy and Buck, and even Fred Rockwell, were doing more work than ever before.

Jess knew that Greg Martin had been diving in the cove and around the *Sea Lark,* but to his disappointment he never was allowed in the skiff, which attended him. When the *Sea Lark*'s engine was running well, and they went out among the islands, perhaps they would take him along, too.

Jess saw little of the Indians. They were seldom around the house and never near the workmen. The red skiff remained on the beach. The men used it whenever they wished, and Mr. Raven did not protest.

One day Grandmother said, "How is Cory? I miss the child."

"I don't see much of her," Jess answered.

"There's going to be a church sale next Wednesday. We're going, and I'd like to ask Cory to come along, too."

"I don't think she'd like to go to a church sale."

"Nonsense," Grandmother said. "There'll be candy and cake and ice cream. I never knew a child who didn't like those treats. If her father will send over a dress, I'll get it ready so she'll look especially nice."

## CHAPTER TEN

# Church Sale

Cory's simple red-and-white dress was washed, starched, and pressed by Grandmother, and her sneakers were scrubbed as clean as new. Grandmother brushed her hair into two neat braids that hung over her shoulders. Cory looked so different, Jess thought, from the ragged urchin with tangled hair in the tattered dungarees. Now she looked like a little lady. Even the Reverend Wiley was surprised when he picked them up to take them to the fair.

"Why, what a pretty child you are, Cordelia," he said in astonishment.

A few cars were parked by the hall, and the doors were wide open. Some ladies were leaving, carrying parcels and talking among themselves.

Grandmother thanked Reverend Wiley as he let them out. "I'm glad you could come, Mrs. Manning," he said. "We worked very hard to get this fair under way. The church needs the money. I think you'll find many lovely things, and there are some for the children as well. Now I must go on to the parsonage."

"Jess, I want you to look out for Cory as if she were your sister," Grandmother told him. "There's some needlework I want to see myself, but there are other things that will interest you."

The big hall was filled with tables piled high with goods, mostly quilts, needlework, pillow slips, and pot holders. Other tables held cakes, round, square, or oblong ones, pans of fudge, chocolate or maple, and many kinds of cookies. On some of the tables there were great buckets of flowers that accented the room with color and had a lovely scent.

It was noon, and only a few customers were present. A woman in charge stood behind each table. As soon as they entered the hall, Jess sensed a change. The people all knew the Mannings. They spoke to Grandmother and to Jess, and then fell silent when they noticed Cory.

"Come on." Jess led Cory to the table where they were selling homemade ice cream. He always visited this one first. Two girls already were waiting to be served. The same thing happened at the ice-cream table. Mrs. Grey said, "Hello, Jess. A nice day for ice cream." Then she became silent when she noticed Cory.

"I'm going to have a double chocolate cone," Jess said. "What'll you have, Cory?"

"The same," Cory said shyly.

Mrs. Grey scooped up the ice cream without comment, but the other girls withdrew a little, whispering and snickering together. When Mrs. Grey handed the ice cream to Cory, one girl said loud enough for all of them to hear, "Same color as the Injun."

Jess was terribly ashamed, but he didn't know what to do. He looked at Mrs. Grey, who took their money, thanking them. She gave Cory's quarter an extra glance. Her face was as blank as if she had heard nothing.

"Come on," Jess said, and roughly catching Cory by the hand, he led her away. They walked in and out among the tables, looking at the things and eating their ice-cream cones. Cory was quiet.

"I should have kicked them," Jess said, "but they were only stupid little girls."

Most of the tables held little of interest to the children, but Cory stopped suddenly in front of the white elephant table. On it were a variety of small articles that housewives had found in their attic and given to the fair. What was of no use to one person might well be valuable to another. There were needles and hooks, odd rolls of yarn, strange-looking flower vases, and a few pretty cups and plates.

Cory's eyes were on a wooden doll, about six inches high, that lay on the edge of the table. "Look!" she whispered. A customer was pawing through the articles, turning over this and that. She picked up the doll, looked at it, then with a shrug put it down.

When the woman left, Cory's hand reached out for the doll. There was a sharp slap over her fingers. "Keep your hands off the merchandise, little girl!" The saleslady turned a thin, angry face to the child. "People don't want your dirty hands on the things they buy."

"My hands aren't dirty!" Cory protested.

Miss Trim tapped loudly on the bell at the end of the table, and at once Miss Ryder, the president of the Ladies' Aid, turned and came in their direction. A hush fell over the hall. No

one looked directly at the white elephant table, yet everyone seemed to be listening.

Now Grandmother was at the table, too. "Elsa Ryder, I must ask that you apologize to Cordelia. The child has touched nothing but an ice-cream cone, which she paid for."

Miss Ryder's eyes rested on Cory with a

bitter, impersonal hatred. "Perhaps so, Mrs. Manning, but we don't want Indians, and Catholics at that, to come to our fair." A low murmur of approval followed her words.

Grandmother threw down the pillow slip she was holding. "You foolish, deluded people, living in your own tight little world. I'm sorry I ever exposed these children to your bigotry. Sell your things to someone else. Come, children, we'll walk home."

"But Grandmother," Jess said, when they started down the road, "Reverend Wiley said he'd take us home. He wouldn't have stood for that kind of talk."

"Reverend Wiley means well, but it is the women who run the church."

The new moon brought rain. It fell gently, without wind. The fragrance of roses filled the dampness. Blackberry bushes, heavy with wetness, lolled, their blossoms snow-white.

Rain had delayed work at the Bonnet, but

with clearing the activity started again. The engine on the *Sea Lark* was working at last, and the men had taken it for several prolonged cruises around the bay. Jess hoped desperately that he would be allowed to come, but he never was invited. The crew on these trips was restricted to Mr. Rockwell, Mr. Martin, and Mr. Barnes. They always took the air tanks and the wet suit with them, so they must be diving.

"I've watched them from the end of the Bonnet," Cory told Jess. "They go down among the reefs and the islands until they're out of sight, but they always go in the same direction."

Buck Rogers was in good humor that afternoon. "Well, Jess," he said, "we'll be done here soon. They're sailing in a couple of weeks. Mr. Barnes is a fine man, and it's been a good job for us this summer, not too much to do. That Martin guy worked us hard, but what did it matter? We had a good time."

"Are they really leaving in a couple of weeks?" Jess asked Mr. Raven, later in the day.

"That's what they say."

"What will you do?"

"Now that Mr. Barnes has sold the place, he wants us to stay and look after it until the new owner comes. Then maybe we'll go back to the reservation," Mr. Raven said.

CHAPTER ELEVEN

# The Insurance Agent

Saint-John's-wort and steeplebush blossomed beside the road, and summer was no longer young. The final work had been done on the *Sea Lark,* and it looked quite different from the shabby boat that had been moored there four months ago. The new paint gave it a smooth, silky look, and the new cabin looked very large.

The next days were devoted to loading.

Greg Martin and Fred Rockwell packed boxes in the house. Buck and Doddy wheeled them down to the beach, put them into the tender, and rowed them out to the *Sea Lark*. Mr. Barnes was there, waiting to store the boxes below deck.

Visitors came over from Summerport, the six selectmen and the sheriff, to admire the *Sea Lark*. Then one lovely, late summer day, the insurance agent arrived.

Mr. Barnes said to Jess, "Bring that round table out of the shed, will you, and put it on the lawn? Then get a couple of lawn chairs. Pick out ones that are solid. I'm having an important guest, and I don't want an accident."

Jess was bringing out the table and chairs when Bob Burns arrived. Jess knew him slightly. He was a young, thin man with thick, dark hair. New to his job, he was hopeful and eager to please.

"It's such a lovely day, too nice to stay in-

doors," Mr. Barnes said. "I thought we might talk business and have some coffee out here in the sun. Go and tell Kathy May, will you, Jess? Then you can do some clipping on that hedge."

Kathy May brought the coffee and some sugared doughnuts, and while the men ate and talked Jess began to work. He couldn't help overhearing what was being said.

"You are new in this business," Mr. Barnes began.

"Yes, my company has never had an agent in the Summerport area. The old Holdfast Company handled all the insurance business. But with so many places being restored and the demand for insurance increasing, they decided to expand to Summerport."

"Giving you a chance to make your mark in the world."

"I don't know as I would say that," Mr. Burns said humbly, but there was a gleam in his eye.

"It pleases me to see a young man so alert. I would enjoy giving you some business, and it is fortunate that I have a few useful connections."

"What do you mean, sir?" Mr. Burns's eyes had a hungry look.

"A company is always pleased when its agent is able to sell large policies to wealthy, reliable people. I know a number of such people; in fact, the ones who are buying this place will undoubtedly wish to increase their insurance, and it would be a pleasure to recommend you."

"That would be very kind, sir," the agent said.

"Now in regard to my affairs, here are the papers on the *Sea Lark*. You see it has cost me a good deal, but it has been worth it. I used fine material, and a lot of labor went into the rebuilding, so you can understand why I want it so well insured. I have a good deal invested in it."

"Oh, I understand perfectly," the agent agreed.

"Here is a list of the cargo and its value. I'm taking with me quite a number of expensive household items. A friend in Florida is interested in buying them."

There was a low murmur of voices as the men bent over the lists. Jess's attention was attracted by the words shouted out, "You call me a liar!"

"Of course not, sir!" Both men were on their feet. Mr. Barnes looked furious, the agent frightened and unhappy. "I merely said it was impossible for me to write so large a policy without first examining the boat and checking the cargo. Surely you know that."

"If the tender were available, we could go out to the *Sea Lark* this minute. But it was leaking so badly, we have had to haul it up to have a plank replaced."

"Oh, well." The agent looked relieved. "It won't take long to make the repair. Then I can go out and make the inspection and issue the policy."

"Unfortunately, they don't have any suitable material at the lumberyard and must order some, so it will take quite a while. But this is all beside the point. I want to get this matter cleared up now, and I have the money here." He brought out a checkbook. "I have many friends in Summerport, the selectmen, the sheriff, and the Reverend Wiley, to name a few, and I have given jobs to those who could not find work. But since you do not have confidence in me, we had best forget the whole affair." He threw the policies onto the table.

"I'm sorry," Mr. Barnes said with deep regret in his voice. "It would have been such an excellent start for you. There is another insurance company here, you know."

"Wait! Wait, Mr. Barnes!" The agent had grown quite pale. "I realize that I should make an inspection before issuing a policy, but under the circumstances and because of the good reputation you have in town, I'll do business with you anyway. Now let's see," he said, picking up the papers from the table.

As the men lowered their voices, Jess returned to the clipping. That was funny, he thought. Why hadn't Mr. Barnes suggested they use the red skiff to go out to the *Sea Lark*?

"They're sailing Monday," Jess told Grandmother. "Doddy and Buck will be finished tomorrow."

"When will you be done?"

"I'm going to stay on until Sunday and help Mr. Rockwell close the place up. Mr. Barnes and Mr. Martin are going away today, but they're coming back on Monday for the *Sea Lark.*"

"I'm sorry they're going, but I'm glad things turned out as well as they did. Since Mr. Barnes has a buyer for the place, everything will be fine. At one time I thought the boat never would be ready, not with the men he had working on it. Buck and Doddy must have done a job after all."

"I'm sorry to see Mr. Barnes go, too. I had a good time," Jess said.

Kathy May's job ended first. "We'll do our own cooking now," Mr. Barnes said.

Doddy and Buck put the finishing touches on the *Sea Lark*. Mr. Barnes paid them and wished them luck.

"Sure was a good job," Buck said. "Sure glad to have it, too."

"And I was happy to have you," Mr. Barnes answered.

There was a sense of friendliness, a sense of a job well done. Even toward Buck and Doddy, Jess felt a sense of comradeship.

Sunday afternoon the Bonnet seemed strangely still, the sound of hammers, the shouts of workmen silenced at last. The *Sea Lark* swung at her mooring, the tender beside her. The red skiff was not in sight.

Jess helped Mr. Rockwell with the last of

the work, closing up the house. Fred Rockwell put on the storm doors, shutting the blinds on the windows, and Jess carried the nails and held the ladder. For once the man worked briskly. He reminded Jess of a horse, who, remembering its dinner, is in a hurry to get home. The house had resumed its cold, blank look.

"Well, we're finished." Fred Rockwell looked at his watch. "I'll get my bags and drive over to Summerport for dinner. I'm sorry to be going. I had a good time here. Oh yes, John left this check for you. He was pleased with your work."

"Thanks," Jess said, smiling.

He put the check into his pocket, but he didn't go home. Instead he went around to the servants' quarters. The door was open, but no one was there.

Perhaps the Ravens had gone clamming or were down on the point picking berries. Jess followed the path past Backside Cove. The little field was empty. A few scraps of timber lay around on the trampled grass. He walked on out to the end of the Bonnet.

There he found Cory down on her knees picking blueberries. "Want to help?" she asked. "There's another bucket."

"Seems quiet, doesn't it?" Jess scooped up a handful of berries. "Mr. Rockwell is going this afternoon. Then you and your father will be the only ones here. We can really have fun then."

"We won't be here either," Cory said.

"But I thought you were staying until the new owner came. Maybe your father can keep his job as caretaker."

"No, we're going just as soon as Mr. Barnes gets back."

"But why? Now the troublemakers have gone."

"Papa says trouble stays here."

"Your father said that before," Jess remembered. "But there hasn't been any trouble.

The *Sea Lark* is ready, and they're sailing tomorrow. What could go wrong now?"

"Jess, Papa overheard Mr. Barnes and Mr. Martin talking. He didn't understand what they meant, but it worried him."

"What did they say?"

"Mr. Barnes said, 'Everything has worked out perfectly, Greg,' and then Mr. Martin said, 'She's covered for plenty, and the fools will never know it.' What did they mean?"

"I don't know, but I don't see how it's anything to worry about."

"But Papa said it was the way they said it, as if they were getting away with something and were pleased about it."

"I don't see why your father thought that," Jess said.

"Well, the last few weeks they've been doing a lot of cruising with the *Sea Lark*."

"So what? Probably they were practicing for the big cruise."

"Mr. Martin was diving," Cory said slowly.

"We know that, because he always took his diving things with him. Mr. Barnes is the only one who goes with him, and they always go in the same direction."

Jess thought for a long moment. "Have you or your father ever been aboard the *Sea Lark*?"

"No."

"Neither have I."

Cory said, "The sheriff and some of the selectmen went aboard once to look at it. Lots of people from Summerport have come over to the cove to see it, but I don't think any of them have been cruising on it, even Mr. Hawthorn and Mr. Rogers."

Truth burst upon Jess like a light. "I know what's happened," he cried. "They've found sunken treasure! I bet Mr. Martin found it while he was diving. That's what's really in those boxes they loaded aboard the *Sea Lark*. That's why they always went in the same direction and why they always went alone. They didn't want anyone to know they'd found it."

"Sunken treasure! In Maine! Where did it come from?" Cory was unbelieving.

"A pirate ship that sank in a storm. Captain Kidd's, maybe. I think he sailed up this way. I bet Mr. Martin had a map that showed where it sank. That's the reason he brought his diving equipment."

"But now that they have it, why won't they tell anyone about it?"

"They're going to take it out of state when they sail. Maybe there's a law against that, so they don't want anyone to find out."

Cory was still doubtful. "I don't believe it. Papa never said anything about sunken treasure. Still, they've been awfully careful not to have anyone aboard, and Mr. Barnes told Papa to be sure no one came near the boat while he was gone."

"I bet that's what they meant about having enough to cover her. They meant they'd found enough treasure to pay for all the work on the *Sea Lark*," Jess explained.

"If they found real treasure, it would be worth a lot more than the old *Sea Lark.*" Cory was becoming interested.

"I wish I could go aboard the boat and look around," Jess said slowly.

"You can't do that! No one is allowed on it."

"But no one is there now, so they'd never know. Where is the red skiff?"

"Papa hid it, so no one would use it now. He wouldn't let you go out there, though."

"I guess not. So we'll never know what they found. I wish I had a skiff of my own."

Cory ate a handful of blueberries, and then said cautiously, "Could you come back late this afternoon?"

"Yes. I think Grandma will let me. Why?"

"Papa's going to take an order of blueberries over to Mrs. Wiley's late in the afternoon. That's why I'm picking them. I know where Papa hid the red skiff, and while he's gone, there'd be time enough to row out to the *Sea Lark.* It wouldn't take long for you to see what's aboard, and then we can row back and put the skiff away. No one will ever know."

Jess stared at her.

"Well, Papa never actually told me not to use the skiff," Cory said defensively.

"All right, I'll come. Where will I find you?"

"I'll be waiting with the skiff in Backside Cove."

# CHAPTER TWELVE

# Aboard the *Sea Lark*

Grandmother welcomed the check. "So the place is closed now. No one over there but the Ravens."

"Yes. Could I go over after supper? I've been so busy I haven't seen much of them."

"Of course, you may."

It was a lovely late summer afternoon when Jess and Tatters followed the dirt road that wound through the woods. Robins were singing loudly for rain. "Cheer-up, cheer-up, cheer-ree!" A few mosquitoes slipped out of the shadows. Jess slapped at them absent-mindedly, his thoughts on other things.

Greg Martin must have discovered sunken treasure. That could be the only answer to the strange behavior of the owner of the *Sea Lark*. True, Jess never had heard of any pirate ships lost in the bay, but he had read stories of finding sunken treasure. Why couldn't it be discovered on the Maine coast as well as anywhere else?

But why were the men so silent about it, now that it was safely aboard? Perhaps they were afraid someone might steal it; the state might even claim it. Jess didn't blame them, and he didn't expect any of the treasure either. He just wanted to look at it. He wanted to be able to say, "You know that treasure Mr. Barnes and his friend found? Well, I was the only person in Summerport who got a look at it!"

The house loomed up, still and dark against the glorious western sky. The sun already was reaching for the hills. They would have to hurry to reach the *Sea Lark* while it was still light enough to see. Jess followed the path down to the cove. The water was at half

tide and rising, and the flats were touched with brightness. A few gulls circled, calling mournfully.

Cory was waiting in the red skiff. Tatters went splashing through the muck, but Jess sent her back, saying, "You can't come,

Tatters! You're too much trouble. Go back and wait. Sit!"

Cory was pushing on the oars to keep the skiff from going aground. "Why were you so slow? It's going to be dark before long, and you won't be able to see anything. Papa will be home, too."

Jess waded out to the skiff. "I'll row. I can row faster than you."

"All right." Cory crawled into the bow, turning the oars over to Jess. He rowed very well, and the skiff moved quickly out into the calm cove. It was only a short distance to the mooring. The cove was very still; only the gulls wheeled overhead. Tatters sat obediently on the banking.

They rounded the stern of the boat, and Jess looked up at the gold letters, *Sea Lark, Summerport, Maine*. Cory caught hold of the side of the boat, but the face she turned to Jess was troubled.

"Do you really think it's all right to go

aboard, Jess? I'm afraid Papa won't like it."

"Of course, it's all right." Jess was not going to be stopped now that he had gone this far. "I'm just going to look at the treasure. I'm not going to touch it. Besides, no one will ever know." He climbed into the boat. "You wait here. I'll be back in a minute."

He moved forward into the open cabin. There was little of interest there—some sailing charts, life jackets, and an oilskin. Everything was very neat and tidy. The door leading belowdecks was closed, and for a dreadful moment Jess thought it might be locked. Then he saw that it was held by nothing more complicated than a series of hooks and latches.

Suddenly on the shore Tatters began barking, or rather she began yodeling. Her fear of the water and the fact that her master had ventured so far on it tore her very soul. "Oh! Oh! Oh! Oh! Oh!" she bellowed.

Jess popped into sight. "Shut up!" he yelled.

"Oh! Oh! Oh!"

"Go back and stay with her, Cory. She'll have all of Summerport over here if she keeps on. When I'm ready, you can row back and get me."

Cory pushed off, taking the oars and working them clumsily, but once the skiff got under way, she rowed well. Jess watched her for a second and then returned to the cabin.

Tatters was quiet, and now Jess had time to begin the search. The cabin was as empty as the deckhouse, and it had the same deserted feeling. "I thought they'd have more things than this aboard," Jess said aloud. "You wouldn't think they were going beyond Summerport."

When Jess noticed the flashlight on the shelf at the head of the bunk, he was delighted, for it was growing dark in the cabin. The light showed little: two bunks, neatly made up, and a sweater thrown into a corner. The galley that opened off the cabin was neat and tidy also, but there was nothing but a couple of cans of beans in the cupboard. Where were the boxes that held the treasure, the boxes Jess had seen brought aboard the *Sea Lark*?

Then he noticed a crack in the floorboards of the cabin and pulled away a floor mat, revealing a trapdoor. Of course, they would store the treasure in the hold, not leave it around in plain sight in the cabin. The door was bolted, but not locked, and a large iron ring served as a handle. Jess slipped the bolt, opened the trapdoor, and looked down a short ladder into a very black hole.

A cold, damp smell rose, like the bottom of the sea. Jess flashed the light down and saw a row of neatly stacked boxes. The treasure was there! Jess climbed down the ladder. Again he was surprised, for the boxes were not even nailed. He pulled open the top one. It contained a few rocks, the sort found in any field. Jess stared at them. Then he thought, Perhaps they put this box on top to discourage robbers. He pulled out one of the bottom crates and opened it, but it was quite empty.

Everything was very still and damp there in

the hold. He could hear the soft chuckling of the water as it slipped along the planks. Why would they load useless crates on a boat bound for Florida? Jess wondered.

The answer was beyond his understanding. His feet were wet, for the *Sea Lark* was leaking some. Jess looked around him and saw that down there, away from the fresh paint and the new wood of the cabin, the *Sea Lark* looked old and shabby.

Well, the whole affair had been a waste of time, and if he didn't get back so Cory could get the red skiff hidden away, they both would be caught. Jess went up the ladder quickly, glad to be free of the cold, damp smell, closed the door behind him, put the flashlight where he had found it, and went on deck.

The night air was cool with a sweet taste of the sea, but it had grown much darker than he had realized. Making out the shore was difficult, and he could not see Cory or Tatters; Jess wasn't even sure that the red skiff was there.

He was about to shout to Cory when he became aware of the sound of a motor. Another boat had entered the cove and was approaching the *Sea Lark*. Jess slipped back into the cabin. Mr. Barnes wasn't supposed to come until tomorrow. Well, perhaps he had forgotten something, had returned to get it, and then would go away. They hadn't seen him, Jess was sure, but where could he hide until they went away? There was the thump of the boats touching and the sound of men's voices.

The cabin and the galley offered no hiding place, but there was the hold. Jess grabbed the flashlight, opened the hatch, and slipped down the ladder, closing the door behind him. Feet were already stamping on the deck above him, and someone was cursing. They must be hunting for the flashlight.

Jess crawled down behind the empty crates and snapped off the flashlight. The men must have found some kind of a light, for the boards creaked as they went about their work.

Suddenly there came a cough and a rattle,

and a vibration shook the boat. They had started the motor, and the *Sea Lark* was under way. Jess's first thought was to run on deck, but then he would be admitting that not only had he boarded the *Sea Lark,* he had stowed away as well. He didn't like to think what Mr. Barnes might say. He could get into a lot of trouble breaking and entering. But he didn't want to go to Florida either. Jess was caught, as they say, between the devil and the deep sea.

Then he thought, There are no provisions aboard the *Sea Lark*. They couldn't sail all the way to Florida on two cans of beans. They would cross the harbor to Summerport, dock there for the night, and in the morning load the supplies and start out. While they were busy getting them aboard, he might be able to slip off unnoticed. Grandmother wouldn't like what had happened one bit, but he'd rather face Grandmother than Mr. Barnes. Of course, if he was really lucky, the men might leave the boat as soon as it docked, and he could get away and hitchhike home. Then neither Grandmother nor Mr. Barnes would be the wiser.

Jess found a piece of canvas and spread it over the crates to make a dry bed. Quietly he curled up on it, his feet out of the water. The sound of the motor had become a drone, and there was the soft *hush, hush, hush* of the water against the bottom of the boat, sounding like a lullaby. In spite of the dark and the dampness, Jess was not uncomfortable, and he soon dozed off.

# CHAPTER THIRTEEN

# In Danger

Jess's head bumped hard against the planking, and cold, oily water splashed over him. He had rolled off the crates and into the bilge. The motion of the boat had changed, jerking and rolling in the sea, not steady as it was in the calm harbor.

Jess guessed more time had passed than it should have taken to reach Summerport. Perhaps they were not going there after all, but would put into some town down the coast. That would be a disaster for Jess, for he would have to go up and tell them that he was aboard. Suddenly the trapdoor opened, and Jess hid as well as he could. A pool of light on the floor of the hold was coming from above. The motor was cut down to low. Then the light dimmed as a man stepped down onto the ladder.

"Keep circling the Fiddler.' Greg Martin was talking. "Not too close in, John. We don't want to hit it."

Jess was astonished. The Fiddler was a reef, a row of rock teeth just below the surface at ebb tide. There was very deep water on either side of it. At one time it must have been the top of a steep mountain that had sunk beneath the sea. But the Fiddler was far out in the bay. What were they doing out there?

"The tender is all ready." Mr. Barnes was in the cabin. "I didn't put too much in it, just oars, oarlocks, and an oilskin. They'll think we hit the ledge, jumped into the tender, and pushed off. Didn't have time to save anything."

Then he began to laugh. "I was thinking of that young agent. First large policy he's sold, and now the boat's lost. His company won't be happy, but he was so eager to make good and to be in line for all that other business I promised that he took a chance."

"Oh, he'll be all right," Martin said. "Only three of us, Rockwell, you, and I, know that the valuation was false. The company will never find the boat and prove anything, so if he keeps his head and doesn't admit he never checked the *Sea Lark* before insuring, who'll be the wiser? It was bad luck, but bad luck does happen. That's why there's insurance."

"What if he gets rattled and tells?"

"If they ask questions, half the town will swear to our good character—the selectmen, the sheriff, that Indian, and the boy and his grandmother. Buck and Doddy, even the minister, know you were a good employer, and I'm your friend."

"You don't think we'll have any trouble with Rockwell?"

"No, he'll be well paid, and those rogues, Buck and Doddy, were so pleased to get a summer's work that they'll never be suspicious. In fact, they don't have brains enough to suspect anything. The boy was only a kid. He never got close enough to know anything."

"The Indians didn't either. They're not too bright, you know."

"I'll pull that sea cock out now," Martin said. "She'll fill slowly, but we'll get her on the port side of the ledge and leave her. It'll look like an accident. They'll think she hit the ledge, and then slid off. She'll go down in deep water, so there won't be anyone poking around her bones." He came down the ladder.

Jess was panicked. They weren't going on any cruise! They were going to scuttle the *Sea Lark* and collect the insurance money. But what would happen to him? His first thought was to jump up and call to Mr. Martin, "I'm here, too. You'll have to take me with you." But he never moved.

Greg Martin went to the stern of the boat and pushed away some old boards, uncovering a patch of freshly tarred canvas over the planks of the hull. He ripped off the patch with an iron bar, exposing a large metal ring sunk into a plank. He slipped the iron bar into the metal ring and pulled hard. A circle of planking came away, and there was the gurgle of flowing water. Greg Martin turned abruptly and went up the ladder.

If I don't yell, I'll drown, Jess thought. But they'll never take me ashore now, not with what I know. They'll let me drown anyway.

Martin had left the trapdoor open, so that the boat would fill more quickly, and a patch of light fell into the hold. The engine had stopped, and there was the scraping sound of the tender being launched. The gurgle from the sea cock was muffled now, but the flow of water had increased. Jess's feet were soaked, and water splashed around the crates.

His first effort was to replace the sea cock, but already the water was deep over the hole. He found the plug, but he was not strong enough to push back against the flowing water. He scrambled up into the cabin, then closed and bolted the trapdoor. Shutting it would not save the boat, but it might slow its sinking.

Somewhere out in the dark, Martin's voice spoke, "She's starting to settle, John. Let's get going."

"Shouldn't we stick around and see what happens?"

"We know what'll happen, and it's a long row to Eagle Island."

Jess put out the flashlight. Luckily he hadn't come onto the deck with it, for if they had seen a light moving about the *Sea Lark,* they would have returned.

Jess knew the men had taken the only

tender, but there must be other things aboard the boat that would float. He might be able to build a raft, and surely there must be life jackets. It was a clear, starlit night, and when his eyes became used to the dim light, he had no trouble finding his way around the deck. There was nothing there, however, that would be of any use in building a raft.

Even the cabin, when he dared use the flashlight, had nothing to offer. Then he saw the ship-to-shore phone. Of course, they had one. Everyone who went cruising did, but he had forgotten. Jess had no idea how to use the equipment, but he had to learn fast. A call might bring help in time. He pressed the button marked *on,* but nothing happened. The ship-to-shore, like everything else aboard the *Sea Lark* had been added for appearance, not for use.

A little water was seeping up through the floorboards of the cabin. He would have to find a life jacket; there was nothing else.

He was hunting for the jacket when there came a scraping sound. The *Sea Lark* shivered, then slowly tipped to port. Jess caught hold of the bunk for support, but the boat didn't tip anymore. It moved forward slightly, grating loudly on something, and then came to a stop. The ebbing tide rippled around it, and waves splashed against it, but the boat did not move.

The *Sea Lark* was aground. The southwest wind had freshened and pushed the boat back onto the Fiddler. But how long would it remain there?

The ebbing tide might cause the boat to settle more firmly on thc ledge, or it might make it tip and slip off into the deep grave, where the owners had planned that it go. Certainly the rising tide and the increased wind would free it for destruction.

Jess now had time to think. Could he find some rope and lash the couple of deck chairs into a rude raft? If he had remembered to bring that iron bar up from the now flooded hold, he might have been able to pry some boards off the cabin. He searched the cupboards and under the bunks without finding anything that would be of help to him. Then he went out onto the deck.

The night was very still; only the gurgle of the water around the boat could be heard. The stars were brilliant, the great constellation Scorpio with its blood-red heart sprawled across most of the southern sky. Overhead, like a road, the Milky Way divided and ran in two paths over the horizon. Out in the night a loon called, a quivering, tragic laughter. Jess shivered, and then suddenly he heard a motor.

Somewhere in the dark there was a boat, perhaps a fisherman making his way home. If only he could attract his attention! But if he used the flashlight, the men in the tender might see it, too! Then, like a white finger, a searchlight reached out, fumbling in the

darkness. It was too far starboard to touch the *Sea Lark*.

They were searching for him! Cory must have told Grandmother what had happened. Jess grabbed the flashlight and holding it high in the air began flashing it, on and off, on and off. The finger of light moved, groping across the night and touched the white cabin of the *Sea Lark*. It held there, and the boat approached steadily.

It was big, much larger than any fisherman's. The motor slowed, and a voice shouted, "This is the Coast Guard cutter *Skidakat*. How badly are you damaged? Do you need help?"

"We're on the Fiddler," Jess shouted. His voice sounded high and squeaky. "We're going to sink! Please take me off!"

There was the sound of a boat being lowered, and the officer called again, "What boat is this?"

"It's the *Sea Lark*. I'm Jess Manning."

"Where is John Barnes?"

"He's gone. They've both gone. They were going to scuttle the boat. Please get me off," Jess pleaded.

The tender edged alongside the *Sea Lark,* and two officers climbed aboard. "Take it easy, son. It's all right. Tom, go below and take a look at things." He put his jacket around the shivering boy. "Tell me what happened."

Jess tried to tell the story clearly, but he was hungry and tired and the wet coldness in his feet seemed to have penetrated his whole body.

"The kid's right." Tom had come up on deck. "The sea cock's open, and the hold is half full of water. I don't know how much damage has been done to the hull."

"We'll take the kid back onto the cutter. He's exhausted. Then we'll see if we can pump the boat out. Better contact the police and the insurance agent. They'll be interested in this. Do you have any idea where those men were headed, kid?"

"They said something about Eagle Island."

Everyone aboard the *Skidakat* was very busy for the next few hours, making calls, getting the pumps to work on the *Sea Lark,* that is, everyone but Jess. He sat in the galley, wrapped in a blanket, drinking hot chocolate and feeling dead tired. "How did you find me?" he asked at last. "Did Cory tell you?"

"Cory? It was your grandmother who called in that you were missing, but I guess an Indian told her what direction the boat went. Now you better lie down and take a nap."

Jess was asleep as soon as he touched the bunk.

The sound of his grandmother's voice awoke him. I've overslept. I haven't milked the cow! Jess thought, and he jumped up so quickly that he bumped his head on the frame of the bunk above him. A patch of sunlight fell down the open hatchway, and Jess pulled aside the blanket that was wound around him and scrambled up the ladder. He ran right into his grandmother's arms.

"Oh, Jesse, Jesse." She patted his head awkwardly. "Why did you do such a brave and foolish thing? Why didn't you tell me something was wrong?"

"But I didn't know what they were going to do! Didn't Cory tell you?" Then he caught sight of Cory standing there beside Grandmother. "That's how you found me, isn't it? Cory knew where to look."

Cory stared at him with her great, dark eyes. "I told Papa what had happened. The boat went in the same direction it's been going all summer. Papa went and told your grandma, and she told these men."

For the first time Jess looked around him, at the Summerport harbor, the docks and the boats. "Where's the *Sea Lark*?"

"We lost her," the Coast Guard captain said.

"We tried pumping, but she had a hole torn through the bottom, and before the tug could get there, she slipped off into deep water. She's where they wanted her all right, but it's not going to do them much good now that we have a witness as to what happened. It's lucky we found you when we did, son."

"Where is Mr. Raven?" Jess crawled out of his grandmother's embrace.

"He's on the dock with Reverend Wiley," she said. "Mr. Wiley brought me over to Summerport."

Jess started down the gangplank with Cory behind him. "What did you tell them?" Jess asked her. "Why did Grandma say how brave I was when I only went aboard looking for that silly treasure?"

"I didn't say anything about treasure. I just told them you went aboard, because you thought something was wrong."

"Oh." Jess thought for a second. "But Cory, that makes me a hero!"

"Good morning, Jesse. We are so thankful that you're safe," Reverend Wiley said, ending his conversation with a Coast Guard officer. "You'll be glad to know they picked up those criminals on Eagle Island. I always thought there was something strange about that man, John Barnes."

"He never said that before," Jess whispered, as they went on up the dock. "He thought Mr. Barnes was wonderful. I liked him, too. I'm sorry it happened."

Mr. Raven was standing beside an old truck, looking out across the harbor toward the Bonnet. He smiled when he saw the children and reached out his hand to Jess. "I'm glad you are safe."

"I wouldn't be if it weren't for you. You're the one who should get the praise."

"Praise doesn't matter as long as you are safe."

"Things will be different now," Jess said. "We can forget all this trouble and have a good time."

"We're going away, Jess," Cory said. For the first time Jess saw the big canvas bag in the back of the truck, the blanket, and the orange crate with one black paw protruding through the slats. Jet gave a hopeless dig for freedom.

"I have a job cutting pulp in the woods north of here," Mr. Raven said. "It is work I like."

"Do you really want to go, Cory?"

The girl looked at him a moment, and then nodded her head. "Yes, I would rather go back to the good Sisters. I miss them. They are the people I know. I can go to school in the winter and be with Papa in the summer. But I wish you were coming with us, Jess!"

The truck driver, a dark-haired young man, came out of one of the buildings. "Come on, Injun," he said, not unkindly. "We've got a long drive ahead of us. The kid can ride in back on the blankets. You can look after your kitty, little girl."

Jess waved until they were out of sight.

* * *

"Grandma," Jess said that night, "why did Mr. Barnes do that? I liked him. Why couldn't he have lived on the Bonnet and used the *Sea Lark* for cruising?"

"And lived happily ever after? That happens only in fairy tales, Jess. Mr. Barnes wanted money, and he thought he had found a safe, if dishonest, way of getting it. He never counted on your being there."

"Cory and her father, why couldn't people like them?"

"People are slow to change, Jess. Perhaps most of the people in Summerport don't really want to change. Cory and her father left you a present, Jess, the red skiff. They brought it over this morning. Cory said it belonged to you, because you helped her find it."

Jess remembered that January storm. "I'll never see them again." He felt like bawling.

"Never is a long time," his grandmother said gently. "You'll see them again. I have no doubt of that. You've grown this summer,

Jesse. You must see that happiness doesn't come every day. So when happy things do happen, we must take them and hold them in our hearts. Then as long as we live, we can look back and remember them and be happy."

## ABOUT THE AUTHOR

Born in Castine, Maine, Elizabeth Ladd has spent almost her entire life on the Maine island of Islesboro, one of the largest of the Penobscot Bay islands. As an only child, Miss Ladd had few playmates, but many pets. Long before she could read she was interested in books, and her mother read to her by the hour. Library facilities were limited, and her parents built up a library of children's classics for her. When she began to make up her own stories her mother wrote them down. "They were terrible stories," Miss Ladd says, "but I was certain I was going to be an author." After her mother's death she shared with her father the work and planning of their farm. The sea is only a mile away, and in summer clamming and fishing were added to their activities. During the long winter evenings she read a great deal and also began to write. Her first book, *Enchanted Island,* was published in 1953. Since her father's death she has been managing the farm alone. Besides her chickens, she has a number of cats, some white Peking ducks, guinea hens, Bantams, and white rabbits. The neighbor's children, who have the run of the farm in summer, say it is almost as good as a zoo. It is no accident that creatures of the sea, cats, and the vagaries of nature figure importantly in her books.